Lorenzo barely ⟨...⟩ guttural rasp as his own voice. Letting go of the pan, he took hold of her upper arms, wrenching her round. He could feel the heat coming off her damp, voluptuous body, and as he touched her she gave a shivery gasp, jerking beneath his cold, wet hands.

That was what did it—what tore through his iron self-control. That shiver of sensual awareness seemed to reverberate through his own body and galvanize him into actions he couldn't control. Suddenly he was pulling her against him as their mouths met and their lips parted, and he was running his slippery hands over her bare back beneath her hot, vanilla-scented hair, dripping cold water on her burning skin.

The kiss was hungry, devouring, urgent. She moved round so she was leaning with her back against the sink, her fingers grasping his shoulders. Lorenzo could feel the jut of her hipbones against his, rising, pressing against his thudding body. His arousal was so sudden, so intense, it was almost painful. He fumbled for the bow at the back of her apron, stretched to breaking point as his fingers moved across her bare, satin-smooth back. He wanted to have her now, standing up against the sink....

As if she'd read his mind she shifted slightly, tearing her lips from his for a moment as she hoisted herself upwards so that she was half sitting on the edge of the worktop. The movement made a little space between them, and without the bewitching ecstasy of her mouth on his, her hot body pressed against him, Lorenzo was pierced through with sudden chilling awareness.

*What the hell was he doing?*

### *From glass slippers to silk sheets*

Our brilliant new miniseries!

Once upon a time there was a humble housekeeper. Proud but poor, she went to work for a charming and ruthless rich man!

She thought her place was below stairs, but her gorgeous boss had other ideas.

He didn't want her in the kitchen, polishing the silver.

He didn't want her in the lounge, plumping the cushions.

He didn't want her in the library, dusting the books....

Her place was in the bedroom, between his luxurious silk sheets.

Stripped of her threadbare uniform, buxom and blushing in his bed, he'll show her that a woman's work has never been so much fun!

Coming in May—another At His Service story:

*The Prince's Chambermaid*

by

Sharon Kendrick

# India Grey

## POWERFUL ITALIAN, PENNILESS HOUSEKEEPER

AT HIS
*Service*

TORONTO • NEW YORK • LONDON
AMSTERDAM • PARIS • SYDNEY • HAMBURG
STOCKHOLM • ATHENS • TOKYO • MILAN • MADRID
PRAGUE • WARSAW • BUDAPEST • AUCKLAND

Recycling programs
for this product may
not exist in your area.

ISBN-13: 978-0-373-12886-0

POWERFUL ITALIAN, PENNILESS HOUSEKEEPER

First North American Publication 2010.

Copyright © 2009 by India Grey.

www.eHarlequin.com

**Printed in U.S.A.**

**All about the author...**
*India Grey*

A self-confessed romance junkie, **INDIA GREY** was just thirteen years old when she first sent off for the Harlequin® writers' guidelines. She can still recall the thrill of getting the large brown envelope with its distinctive logo through the letter box, and subsequently whiled away many a dull school day staring out of the window and dreaming of the perfect hero. She kept these guidelines with her for the next ten years, tucking them carefully inside the cover of each new diary in January, and beginning every list of New Year's resolutions with the words *Start Novel*. In the meantime she gained a degree in English literature and language from Manchester University, and in a stroke of genius on the part of the Gods of Romance, met her gorgeous future husband on the very last night of their three years there.

The past fifteen years have been spent blissfully buried in domesticity, and heaps of pink washing generated by three small daughters, but she has never really stopped daydreaming about romance. She's just profoundly grateful to have finally got an excuse to do it legitimately!

For Debbie and Alyson, without whose wit, wisdom and daily conferences in the school car park this book would have been written much more quickly (but at further risk to my sanity).

# CHAPTER ONE

*ELIGIBLE bachelor.*

Sarah came to a standstill in the middle of the car park, her fist tightening around the envelope in her hand.

She had to find an *eligible bachelor.* As an item in a scavenger hunt.

Since she'd conspicuously failed to find one of those in real life, her chances of success tonight seemed slim.

Beyond the rows of shiny Mercedes and BMWs parked outside Oxfordshire's trendiest dining pub, the fields and streams and woodland coppices she had grown up amongst lay golden and peaceful in the low summer sun. She gazed out across them, the envelope still clutched in her hand as adrenaline fizzed through her bloodstream and her mind raced.

She didn't have to go in there; didn't have to take part in this stupid scavenger hunt for her sister's hen weekend; didn't have to be the butt of everyone's jokes all the time—Sarah, nearly thirty and on the shelf. No, she knew these fields like the back of her hand, and could remember loads of good hiding places.

Thrusting a hand through her tangled curls, she sighed. Hiding up a tree might be considerably more appealing than going into a pub and having to find an eligible bachelor, but at the age of twenty-nine it was slightly less socially acceptable. And she couldn't really spend the rest of her life hiding. Everyone said she had to get back out there and face it all again, for Lottie's sake. Children needed two parents, didn't they? Girls needed fathers. Sooner or later she should at least try to find someone to fill the rather sudden vacancy left by Rupert.

The prospect made her feel cold inside.

Later. Definitely later, rather than sooner. Right now she was going to—

The doors to the bar opened and a group of city types spilled out, laughing and slapping each other on the back in an excess of beery camaraderie. They barely glanced at her as they walked past, but almost as an afterthought the last one dutifully held the door open for her.

Hell. There was no way she could not go in now. They'd think she was some kind of weirdo whose idea of a good night out was hanging around in a pub car park. Stammering her thanks, she slipped into the dim interior of the bar, shoving the envelope into the back pocket of her jeans with a shaking hand.

In the years since she'd moved away from Oxfordshire The Rose and Crown had transformed itself from a tiny rural pub with swirly-patterned carpets and faded hunting prints on the nicotine-stained walls to a temple of good taste, with reclaimed-oak floors, exposed brickwork and a background soundtrack of achingly trendy 'mood music' obviously intended to help the clientele of stockbrokers and barristers feel instantly 'chilled out'.

It made Sarah feel instantly on edge. And about ninety years old.

She was about to turn round and walk straight out again when some latent sense of pride stopped her. It was ridiculous, she thought impatiently; she was used to doing things on her own. She put up shelves on her own. She did her income-tax form without help. She brought up her daughter completely singlehandedly. She could surely walk into a bar and get herself a drink.

Murmuring apologies, she slipped through the press of bodies into a space by the bar and glanced nervously around. The doors were open onto the terrace and she could see Angelica and her friends gathered round a big table in the centre. It would have been impossible to miss them. Even in this place, theirs was easily the noisiest, most glamorous group and was clearly attracting the attention of every single male within eyeing-up distance. They were all wearing T-shirts provided by Angelica's chief bridesmaid, a gazelle-like girl called Fenella, who worked in PR and who was also responsible for the scavenger-hunt idea. The T-shirts had 'Angelica's final fling' emblazoned across the front in pink letters, and Fenella had only had them made in a size 'small'.

Sarah tugged at hers surreptitiously, desperately trying to make it cover the strip of bare flesh above the waistband of her too-tight jeans. Perhaps if she'd actually stuck to her New Year diet she'd be out there now, laughing, tossing back cocktails and shiny hair and collecting eligible bachelors with the best of them. Hell, if she was a stone lighter perhaps she wouldn't even need an eligible bachelor because maybe then Rupert wouldn't have felt the need to get engaged to a glacial blonde Systems Analyst called Julia. But too many nights spent on the sofa while Lottie was asleep, with nothing but a bottle of cheap wine and the biscuit tin for company, had meant she'd failed to lose even a couple of pounds.

She'd definitely try extra-hard between now and the wedding, she vowed silently, trying to make her way to the bar. It was taking place in the ruined farmhouse Angelica and Hugh had bought in Tuscany and were currently having lavishly done up, and Sarah had a sudden mental image of Angelica's friends floating around the newly landscaped garden in their delicious little silken dresses, while she lurked in the kitchen, covering her bulk with an apron.

Fenella passed her now, on the way back from the bar with a handful of multicoloured drinks sprouting umbrellas and cherries. She eyed Sarah with cool amusement. 'There you are! We'd almost given up on you. What are you drinking?'

'Oh—er—I'm just going to have a dry white wine,' said Sarah. She should really opt for a slimline tonic, but hell, she needed something to get her through the rest of the evening.

Fenella laughed—throwing her head back and producing a rich, throaty sound that had every man in the vicinity craning round to look. 'Nice try, but I don't think so. Look in your envelope—it's the next challenge,' she smirked, sliding through the crowd towards the door.

With her heart sinking faster than the *Titanic,* Sarah slid the envelope from her pocket and pulled out the next instruction.

She gave a moan of dismay.

The beautiful, lithe youth behind the bar flickered a glance in her direction and gave a barely perceptible jerk of his head, which she took as a grudging invitation to order. Her heart was hammering uncomfortably against her ribs and she could feel the heat begin to rise to her cheeks as she opened her mouth.

'I'd like a Screaming Orgasm, please.'

The voice that came from her dry throat was low and cracked, but sadly not in a good way. The youth lifted a scornful eyebrow.

'A what?'

'A Screaming Orgasm,' Sarah repeated miserably. She could feel the press of bodies behind her as other people jostled for a place at the bar. Her cheeks were burning now, and there was an uncomfortable prickling sensation rippling down the back of her neck, as if she was being watched. Which, of course, she was, she thought despairingly. Every one of Angelica's friends had temporarily suspended their own professional flirtation operations and was peering in through the open doors, suppressing their collective mirth.

Well, at least *they* were finding this amusing. The youth flicked back his blond fringe and regarded her with dead eyes. 'What's one of those?' he said tonelessly.

'I don't know.' Sarah raised her chin and smiled sweetly, masking her growing desperation. 'I've never had one.'

'Never had a Screaming Orgasm? Then please, allow me...'

The voice came from just behind her, close to her ear, and was a million miles from the hearty, public-school bray of The

Rose and Crown's usual clientele. As deep and rich as oak-aged cognac, it was infused with an accent Sarah couldn't immediately place, and the slightest tang of dry amusement.

Her head whipped round. In the crush at the bar it was impossible to get a proper look at the man who had spoken. He was standing close behind her and was so tall that her eyes were on a level with the open neck of his shirt, the triangle of olive skin at his throat.

She felt an unfamiliar lurch in the pit of her stomach as he leaned forward in one fluid movement, towering over her as he spoke to the youth behind the bar.

'One shot each of vodka, Kahlua, Amaretto...'

His voice really was something else. Italian. She could tell by the way he said 'Amaretto', as if it were an intimate promise. Her nipples sprang to life beneath the tiny T-shirt.

God, what was she doing? Sarah Halliday didn't let strange men buy her cocktails in pubs. She was a grown woman with a five-year-old daughter and the stretch marks to prove it. She'd been madly in love with the same man for nearly seven years. Lusting after strangers in bars wasn't her style.

'Thanks for your help,' she mumbled, 'but I can get this myself.'

She glanced up at him again and felt her chest tighten. The evening sun was coming from behind him but Sarah had an impression of dark hair, angular features, a strong jaw shadowed with several days of stubble. The exact opposite of Rupert's English, golden-boy good looks, she thought with a shiver. Compelling rather than handsome.

And then he turned and looked back at her.

It felt as if he'd reached out and pulled her into the warmth of his body. His narrowed eyes were so dark that even this close she couldn't see where the irises ended and the pupils began, and they travelled over her face lazily for a second before slipping downwards.

'I'd like to get it for you.'

He said it simply, emotionlessly, as a statement of fact, but there was something about his voice that made the blood throb in her ears, her chest, her too-tight jeans.

'No, really, I can…'

With shaking hands she opened her purse and peered inside, but the chemical reaction that had just taken place in the region of her knickers was making it difficult to see clearly or think straight.

Apart from a handful of small change her purse was virtually empty, and with a rush of dismay she remembered handing over her last five-pound note to Lottie for the swear box. Lottie's policy on swearing was draconian and—since she'd introduced a system of fines—extremely lucrative. Clearly her killer business instinct had come from Rupert. The frustrations of the scavenger hunt this afternoon had cost Sarah dearly.

Now she looked up in panic and met the deadpan stare of the barman.

'Nine pounds fifty,' he said flatly.

*Nine pounds fifty?* She'd ordered a drink, not a three-course meal—she and Lottie could live for a week on that. Faint with horror, she looked down into her purse again while her numb brain raced. When she raised her head again it was to see the stranger hand a note over to the blond youth and pick up the ridiculous drink.

He moved away from the bar, and the crowd through which she'd had to fight a passage fell away for him, like the Red Sea before Moses. Unthinkingly she found herself following him, and couldn't help her gaze from lingering on the breadth of his shoulders beneath the faded blue shirt he wore. He seemed to dwarf every other man in the packed room.

He stopped in the doorway to the terrace and held out the drink to her. It was white and frothy, like a milkshake. A very expensive milkshake.

'Your first Screaming Orgasm. I hope you enjoy it.'

His face was expressionless, his tone dutifully courteous, but as she took the glass from him their fingers touched and Sarah felt electricity crackle up her arm.

She snatched her hand away so sharply that some of the cocktail splashed onto her wrist. 'I doubt it,' she snapped.

The stranger's dark eyebrows rose in sardonic enquiry.

'Oh, God, I'm so sorry,' Sarah said, horrified by her own crassness. 'That sounds so ungrateful after you paid for it. It's just that it's not a drink I'd usually choose, but I'm sure it'll be delicious.' And account for about three days' calorie allowance, she thought, taking a large gulp and forcing herself to look appreciative. 'Mmm…lovely.'

His eyes held her, dark and steady. 'Why did you ask for it if it's not your kind of thing?'

Sarah gave a half-hearted smile. 'I have nothing against screaming orgasms in theory, but,' she held up the envelope, 'it's a scavenger hunt. You have to collect different items on a list. It's my sister's hen weekend, you see…'

*Half-sister. She probably should have explained. Right now he was no doubt wondering which one of the beautiful thoroughbred babes out there she could possibly share a full set of genes with.*

'So I gathered.' He glanced down at her T-shirt and then out into the warm evening, where Angelica and Fenella and their friends had collected a veritable crowd of eligible bachelors and were cavorting conspicuously with them. 'You don't seem to be enjoying it quite as much as the others.'

'Oh, no, I'm having a great time.' Sarah made a big effort to sound convincing. One of Angelica's friends was a holistic counsellor and had told her at lunchtime that she had a 'negative aura'. She took another mouthful of the disgusting cocktail and tried not to gag.

Gently he took the glass from her and put it on the table behind them. 'You are one of the worst actresses that I've come across in a long time.'

'Thanks,' she mumbled. 'There goes my promising career as a Hollywood screen goddess.'

'Believe me, it was a compliment.'

She looked up quickly, wondering if he was teasing her, but his expression was utterly serious. For a moment their eyes locked. The bolt of pure, stinging desire that shot through her took her completely by surprise and she felt the blood surge up to her face.

'So what else is on your list of things to find?' he asked.

'I don't know yet.' She tore her gaze away from his and looked down at the envelope in her hand. 'It's all in here. As you get each item you open up the next envelope.'

'How many have you got so far?'

'One.'

His long, downturned mouth quirked into half a smile, but Sarah noticed that it didn't chase the shadows from his eyes. 'The drink was the first?'

'Actually it was the second. But I gave up on the first.'

'Which was?'

She shook her head, deliberately letting her hair fall over her face. 'It's not important.'

His fingers closed around the envelope in her hand and gently he took it from her. For a second she tried to snatch it back but he was too strong for her and she looked away in embarrassment as he unfolded the paper and read what was written there.

She looked past him into the blue summer evening. Out on the terrace, Fenella was watching her, and Sarah saw her nudge Angelica and smirk as she nodded in Sarah's direction.

'*Dio mio,*' said the man beside her, his husky Italian voice tinged with distaste. 'You have to "collect" an eligible bachelor?'

'Yes. Not exactly my forte.' Angrily Sarah turned away from the curious glances from the terrace and gave a short, bitter laugh. 'I don't suppose you're one, are you?'

The moment she'd spoken she felt her face freeze with embarrassment as she realised how it had sounded. As if she was desperate. And as if she was coming on to him. 'Sorry,' she muttered. 'Let's just pretend that I never asked that—'

'No,' he said tersely.

'Please…' she ducked her head, staring down at the fashionably worn wooden floorboards '…forget it. You don't have to answer.'

'I just did. The answer's no. I am neither a bachelor nor remotely eligible,' he said gravely, reaching out and lifting her chin with his finger, so that she was left with no choice but to look up into his face. His eyes were black and impossible to read. 'But *they* don't know that,' he murmured as he moved his lips to hers.

As ideas went, it probably wasn't his most sensible, Lorenzo thought as he tilted her face up. He saw her dark eyes widen in shock as he brought his mouth down to hers.

But he was bored. Bored and disillusioned and frustrated, and this was as good a way as any of escaping those feelings for a while. Her lips were as soft and sweet as he'd imagined they would be, and as he kissed her with deliberate gentleness he breathed in the clean, artless smell of soap and washing powder.

She was shaking. Her body was rigid with tension, her mouth stayed tightly closed beneath his. Anger at the women on the terrace, who had obviously given her a hard time, churned inside him, adding to the sour disappointment of the day. Instinctively he raised one hand to cradle her face while the other slid beneath the warm tumble of her silken hair and cupped the back of her head.

Patience was one of the things that made him good at his job. The ability to make women relax and release their inhibitions was another. He held her with infinite care, close enough to make her feel cherished, but not so tightly she felt threatened. Gently his fingers caressed the nape of her neck, the secret dip at the base of her skull as his mouth very languidly explored hers.

Triumph shot through him as a soft moan escaped her and felt the stiffness leave her body. Her plump lips parted, her spine arched towards him and then she was kissing him back, with a tentative passion that was surprisingly exciting.

Lorenzo found he was smiling. For the first time in days… *Dio,* months, he was actually smiling, smiling against her mouth at the sheer unexpected sweetness of kissing this woman with the glorious auburn curls and the spectacular breasts and the sad, sad eyes.

He had come to Oxfordshire on a sort of desperate pilgrimage; a search for places that had long existed in his head thanks to a tattered paperback by a little-known author, picked up by chance years ago. The landscape described so lucidly in Francis Tate's beautiful, lyrical novel had haunted him for years, and he had come here in the hope that it might rekindle some spark of the creativity that had died alongside the rest of his emotional life. But the reality of the place was disappointing; a far cry from the gentle, rural paradise Tate depicted in *The Oak and the Cypress.* Lorenzo had discovered a parody of picture-postcard England, bland and soulless.

This woman was the most real, genuine thing he'd come across since he'd arrived here, and probably long before. Emotions played across her face like shadows on a summer day. She didn't conceal anything. Couldn't pretend.

After Tia's prolonged, sophisticated deception he found that profoundly attractive.

And she was actually as sexy as hell. Beneath that self-deprecating insecurity, this girl had depths of heat and passion. He'd kissed her because he felt sorry for her; because she looked sad; because it would cost nothing and mean nothing…

He hadn't expected to enjoy it as much as this.

Lorenzo felt his smile widen as his hands moved down to her curvaceous waist and pulled her against him, desire spiralling down through the pit of his stomach as his fingers met the warm, soft flesh beneath the T-shirt…

She froze. Her eyes flew open, and then suddenly she was pushing him away; stumbling backwards. Her mouth was reddened and bee-stung from his kiss, and above it her dark eyes welled with hurt as they darted wildly in the direction of the whooping, clapping girls on the terrace before coming back to him.

For a second she just stared at him, her face stricken, and then she turned and pushed her way through the crush of bodies towards the door.

It was a joke, of course. That was what hen parties were all about. Jokes. Fun. Flirting. It was just part of all of that.

Pushing through a gap in the hedge at the back of the car park, Sarah felt the thorns scrape at her bare arms and angrily scrubbed the tears from her face with the back of her hand. *Ouch*. It hurt. That was why she was crying. Not because she couldn't take a joke.

Even one as hurtful and humiliating as being kissed in a pub by a complete stranger who couldn't even keep a straight face while he was doing it. God, no. She wouldn't get upset about a silly, harmless thing like that.

Hell, she thought, striding angrily through the waist-high wheat, she was the woman who only a week ago had done the catering for an engagement party and dropped the cake—complete with lighted sparklers—in front of all the guests and the happy couple. One half of which just happened to have been her lover of seven years and the father of her child. Embarrassment and abject shame were old friends of hers. The small matter of being set up to provide hilarious entertainment for her sister's hen party was nothing to Sarah Halliday: the original poster child for humiliation.

The sun was low, dipping down to the horizon, dazzling her through her tears and turning the field into a shimmering sea of gold. Sarah swiped furiously at the wheat in her path, giving vent to the fury and resentment that buzzed through veins that a few moments ago had been thrumming with desire.

That was the worst bit, she thought despairingly. Not that she'd been set up, but that it had felt so wonderful. She was so lonely and desperate that the empty kiss of a stranger had actually made her feel cherished and special and desirable and *good*...

Right up to the moment she'd realised he was laughing at her.

Reaching the brow of the hill, she tipped back her head and took a big, steadying breath. High up in the faded blue sky the pale ghost of the moon hovered, waiting for the sun to finish its flamboyant exit. It made her think of Lottie, and she found that she was smiling as she started walking again, quickening her pace as she descended the hill towards home.

Lorenzo bent to pick up the envelope that she'd dropped in her hurry to get away from him.

Funny, he thought acidly, in all the versions of the story he'd ever read it was a shoe Cinderella left behind when she fled from the ball. He turned it over. Ah. So her name wasn't Cinderella...

It was Sarah.

Sarah. It sounded honest and simple and wholesome, he reflected as he pushed through the crowd towards the door. It suited her.

He strode quickly out into the middle of the dusty lane that ran in front of The Rose and Crown and looked around. To the right, the car park was packed bumper-to-bumper and he half expected to see one of the gleaming BMWs shoot backwards out of its space and accelerate out into the narrow road. But no engine noise shattered the still evening.

There was no sign of her.

Intrigued, he shaded his eyes against the low, flaming sun and turned slowly around, scanning the fields of wheat and hedgerows that unfolded on every side. The air was thick, dusty, hazy with heat and, apart from the distant sound of voices and laughter from the terrace, all was quiet. It seemed she had completely vanished.

He was about to turn and go back inside when a movement in the distance caught his eye. Someone was walking through the field beyond the pub, wading through the rippling wheat with fluid, undulating strides. Unmistakably female, she had her back to him, and the sinking sun lit her riot of curls, giving her an aura of pure gold that would have won any lighting technician an Oscar.

It was her. Sarah.

He felt the deep, almost physical jolt in his gut that he got when he was working and instantly his fingers itched for a camera. This was what he had come here looking for. Here, in front of him, was the essence of Francis Tate's England, the heart and soul of the book Lorenzo had loved for so long, encapsulated by this timeless, sensual image of a girl with the sun in her hair, waist-high in wheat.

On the brow of the hill she paused, tipping back her head and looking up at the pale smudge of moon, so that her hair cascaded down her back. Then, after a moment, she carried on down the slope and disappeared from view.

He let out a long, harsh lungful of air, realising for the first time that he'd been holding his breath as he watched her. He didn't know who this Sarah was or what had made her run out like that, but actually he didn't care. He was just very grateful that she had, because in doing so she'd unwittingly given him back something he thought he'd lost for ever. His hunger to work again. His creative vision.

Which, he thought grimly as he walked back across the road, just left the slightly more prosaic matter of copyright permission.

# CHAPTER TWO

*THREE weeks later.*

Sarah's head throbbed and tiredness dragged at her body, but as she closed her eyes and took a deep inhalation of warm night air she felt her battered spirits lift a little.

*Tuscany.*

You could smell it; a resiny, slightly astringent combination of rosemary and cedar and the tang of sun-baked earth that was a million miles from the diesel smog that hung over London's airless streets at the moment. Britain had been having an extended spell of hot weather that had made the headlines night after night for weeks, but here the heat felt different. It had an elemental quality that stole into your bones and almost forced you to relax.

'You look shattered, darling.'

Across the table her mother's eyes met hers over her glass of Chianti. Sarah smothered a yawn and smiled quickly.

'It's the travelling. I'm not used to it. But it's great to be here.'

She was surprised, as she said the words, to realise how true they were. She'd got so used to dreading Angelica's wedding with all its leaden implications of her own conspicuous failure in so many departments—most notably the 'finding a lifelong partner' one—that she had neglected to take into account how wonderful it would be to come to Italy. The fulfilment of a lifelong dream, from way back when she could afford to have dreams.

'It's great that you're here.' Martha's eyes narrowed shrewdly. 'I think you needed to get away from things because frankly, my darling, you're not looking in great shape.'

'I know, I know…' Aware of her straining waistband, Sarah squirmed uncomfortably. The bonus of having a broken heart was supposed to be that you lost your appetite and the weight fell off, but she was still waiting for that phase to kick in. At the moment she was stuck in the 'bitterness-and-comfort-eating' stage. 'I *am* on a diet, but it's been tough, what with Rupert and work and worrying about money and everything—'

'I didn't mean it like that,' Martha said gently. 'I meant mentally. But if money is difficult, darling, you know Guy and I will help.'

'No!' Sarah's response was instant. 'Really, it's fine. Something will come up.' Her thoughts strayed to the letter she'd had a couple of weeks ago from her father's publishers, the latest in a long line of requests she'd received for film options on *The Oak and the Cypress* in the eleven years since she'd inherited the rights. In the beginning she'd actually taken several of these offers seriously, until bitter experience had taught her that Francis Tate seemed to attract penniless film students with a tendency to bizarre, obsessive psychological disorders. Now, for the sake of her sanity and her burdensome sense of responsibility to her father's memory, she simply refused permission outright.

'How's Lottie doing?' Martha asked now.

Sarah glanced uneasily across at Lottie, who was sitting on Angelica's knee. 'Fine,' she said, hating the defensive note that crept into her voice. 'She hasn't even noticed that Rupert isn't around any more, which makes me realise just what a terrible father he's been. I can't remember the last time he spent time with her.' Latterly most of Rupert's visits to the flat in Shepherd's Bush had been for hasty and singularly unsatisfactory sex in his lunch hour when Lottie was at school. Sarah shuddered now when she thought of his clumsy, careless touch, and his easy excuses about problems at the office and the pressure of work for the evenings and weekends he no longer spent with her. She wondered how long he would have carried on the deceit if she hadn't found him out so spectacularly.

'You're better off without him,' Martha said, as if she'd read Sarah's thoughts. Sarah sincerely hoped she hadn't.

'I know.' She sighed and got to her feet, starting to gather up the plates. 'Really. I know. I don't need a man.'

'That's not what I said.' Martha stood up too, reaching across for the wine, holding the bottle up to the light of the candle and squinting at it to see if there was any left. 'I said without *him*, not without a man in general.'

'I'm happy on my own,' Sarah said stubbornly. It wasn't exactly a lie; she was happy enough. But she only had to think back to the dark, compelling Italian who had kissed her at Angelica's hen party to know that she was also only half-alive. Briskly she moved around the table, stacking crockery, keeping her hands busy. 'You're just missing Guy. You always get ridiculously sentimental when he's not here.'

Guy and Hugh and all his friends weren't arriving until tomorrow, so tonight it was just 'the girls', as Angelica called them. Martha shrugged. 'Perhaps. I'm just an old romantic. But I don't want you to miss your chance at love because you're determined to look the other way, that's all.'

*Fat chance of that,* thought Sarah, carrying the plates back to the kitchen. Her love life was a vast, deserted plain. If anything ever did chance to appear on the horizon she'd be certain to see it. Whether it would stop or not was another matter altogether.

Looming ahead of her through the Tuscan night, the farmhouse was a jumble of uneven buildings and gently sloping roofs. The kitchen was at one end, a low-ceilinged single-storey addition that Angelica said had once been a dairy. Sarah went in and switched the light on, tiredly setting down the pile of plates on the un-rustic shiny marble countertop. Despite being utterly uninterested in cooking, Angelica and Hugh had spared no expense in the creation of the kitchen, and Sarah couldn't quite stamp out a hot little flare of envy as she looked around, mentally comparing it with the tiny, grim galley kitchen in her flat in London.

Crossly she turned on the cold tap and let the water run over her wrists. Heat, tiredness and a glass of Chianti had lowered her defences tonight, making it harder than usual to hold back all kinds of forbidden thoughts. She turned off the tap and went back out into the humid evening, pressing her cool, damp hands against her hot neck, beneath her hair. As she returned to the table Angelica was running through the catalogue of disasters that had beset the renovations.

'…it seems he's absolutely fanatical about having everything as natural and authentic as possible. He confronted our architect with this obscure bit of Tuscan planning law that meant we weren't allowed to put a glass roof on the kitchen, but had to reuse the old tiles. Something to do with maintaining the original character of the building.'

Fenella rolled her eyes. 'That's all very well for him to say, since he lives in a sixteenth-century *palazzo*. Does he expect you to live like peasants just because you bought a farmhouse?'

Martha looked up with a smile as Sarah sat down again. 'Hugh and Angelica have fallen foul of the local aristocracy,' she explained. 'From Palazzo Castellaccio, further up the lane.'

'Aristocracy?' Angelica snorted. 'I wouldn't mind if he was, but he's definitely new money. A film director. Lorenzo Cavalleri, he's called. He's married to that stunning Italian actress, Tia de Luca.'

Fenella was visibly excited. Dropping a celebrity name in front of her had roughly the same effect as dropping a biscuit in front of a dog. 'Tia de Luca? Not any more apparently.' She sat up straighter, practically pricking up her ears and panting. 'There's an interview with her in that magazine I bought at the airport yesterday. *Apparently* she left her husband for Ricardo Marcello, *and* she's pregnant.'

'Ooh, how exciting,' said Angelica avidly. 'Ricardo Marcello's *gorgeous*. Is the baby his, then?'

You'd think they were talking about intimate acquaintances, thought Sarah, stifling another yawn. She knew who Tia de Luca was, of course—everyone did—but couldn't get excited about the complicated love life of someone she would never meet and with whom she had nothing in common. Fenella was clearly untroubled by such details.

'Not sure—from what she said, I think the baby might be the husband's, you know, Lorenzo Whatshisname.' She lowered her voice. 'Have you met him?'

Across the table, Lottie was lolling on her grandmother's knee, her thumb in her mouth. She was obviously exhausted, and Sarah's own eyelids felt as if they had lead weights attached to them; leaning back in her chair, she tipped up her head and allowed herself the momentary luxury of closing them while the conversation ebbed around her.

'No,' Angelica said. 'Hugh has. Says he's difficult. Typical Italian alpha male, all arrogant and stand-offish and superior. We have to keep on the right side of him though, because the church where we're getting married is actually on part of his land.'

'Mmm…' Fenella's voice was warm and throaty. 'He sounds delish. I wouldn't mind getting on the right side of an Italian alpha male…'

Sarah opened her eyes, dragging herself ruthlessly back from the edge of that tempting abyss.

'Come on, Lottie. It's time you were in bed.'

At the mention of her name Lottie struggled sleepily upright, reluctant as ever to leave a party. 'I'm not, Mummy,' she protested. 'Really…'

'Uh-uh.' Lottie had the persuasive powers of a politician, and usually Sarah's resistance in the face of her killer combination of sweetness and logic was pitifully low. But not tonight. A mixture of exhaustion and an odd, restless feeling of dissatisfaction sharpened her tone. 'Bed. Now.'

Lottie blinked up at the sky over Sarah's shoulder. Her forehead was creased up with worry. 'There's no moon,' she whispered. 'Don't they have the moon in Italy?'

In an instant Sarah's edgy frustration melted away. The moon was Lottie's touchstone, her security blanket. 'Yes, they do,' she said softly, 'but tonight it must be tucked up safely behind all the clouds. Look, there are no stars either.'

Lottie's frown eased a little. 'If there are clouds, does that mean it's going to rain?'

'Oh, gosh, don't say that,' laughed Angelica, getting up and coming over to give Lottie a goodnight kiss. 'It better not. The whole point of having the wedding here was the weather. It *never* rains in Tuscany!'

It was going to rain.

Standing at the open window of the study, Lorenzo breathed in the scent of dry earth and looked up into a sky of starless black. Down here the night was hot and heavy, but a sudden breeze stirred the tops of the cypress trees along the drive, making them shiver and whisper that a change was on the way.

*Grazie a Dio.* The dry spell had lasted for months now, and the ground was cracking and turning to dust. In the garden Alfredo had almost used up his barrels of hoarded rainwater, laboriously filling watering cans to douse the plants wilting in the *limonaia,* and in daylight the view of the hillside below Palazzo Castellaccio was as uniformally brown as a faded sepia print.

Suddenly from behind him in the room there came a low gasp of sensual pleasure, and Lorenzo turned round just in time to see his ex-wife's lover bend over her naked body, circling her rosy nipple with his tongue.

Expertly done, he thought acidly as the huge plasma screen above the fireplace was filled with a close shot of Tia's parted lips. Ricardo Marcello was about as good at acting as your average plank of wood but he certainly came to life in the sex scenes, with the result that the completed film—a big-budget blockbuster about the early life of the sixteenth-century Italian scientist Galileo—contained rather more of them than Lorenzo had originally planned. Audiences across the world were likely to leave the cinema with little notion of Galileo as the father of modern science but with a lingering impression of him as a three-times-a-night man who was prodigiously gifted in a Kama Sutra of sexual positions.

With an exhalation of disgust Lorenzo reached for the remote control and hit 'pause' just as the camera was making yet another of its epic journeys over the honeyed contours of Tia's flatteringly lit, cosmetically enhanced body. *Circling the Sun* was guaranteed box-office gold, but it marked the moment of total creative bankruptcy in his own career; the point at which he had officially sold out, traded in his integrity and his vision for money he didn't need and fame he didn't want.

He'd done it for Tia. Because she'd begged him to. Because he *could*. And because he had wanted, somehow, to try to make up for what he couldn't give her.

He had ended up losing everything, he thought bitterly.

As if sensing his mood the dog that had been sleeping curled up in one corner of the leather sofa lifted his head and jumped down, coming over and pressing his long nose into Lorenzo's hand. Lupo was part-lurcher, part-wolfhound, part-mystery, but though his pedigree was dubious his loyalty to Lorenzo wasn't. Stroking the dog's silky ears, Lorenzo felt his anger dissolve again. That film might have cost him his wife, his self-respect and very nearly his creative vision, but it was also the brick wall he had needed to hit in order to turn his life around.

Francis Tate's book lay on the desk beside him and he picked it up, stroking the cover with the palm of his hand. It was soft and worn with age, creased to fit the contours of his body from many years of being carried in his pocket and read on planes and during breaks on film sets. He'd found it by chance in a secondhand bookshop in Bloomsbury on his first trip to England. He had been nineteen, working as a lowly runner on a film job in London. Broke and homesick, and the word *Cypress* on the creased spine of the book had called to him like a warm, thyme-scented whisper from home.

Idly now he flicked through the yellow-edged pages, his eyes skimming over familiar passages and filling his head with images that hadn't lost their freshness in the twenty years since he'd first read them. For a second he felt almost light-headed with longing. It might not be commercial, it might just end up costing him more than it earned but, *Dio,* he wanted to make this film.

Involuntarily, his mind replayed the image of the girl from The Rose and Crown—Sarah—walking through the field of wheat; the light on her bare brown arms, her treacle-coloured hair. It had become a sort of beacon in his head, that image; the essence of the film he wanted to create. Something subtle and quiet and honest.

He wanted it more than anything he had wanted for a long time.

A piece of paper slipped out from beneath the cover of the book and fluttered to the floor. It was the letter from Tate's publisher:

*Thank you for your interest, but Ms Halliday's position on the film option for her father's book* The Oak and the Cypress *is unchanged at present. We will, of course, inform you should Ms Halliday reconsider her decision in the future.*

Grimly he tossed the book down onto the clutter on the low coffee table and went back over to the open window. He could feel a faint breeze now, just enough to lift the corners of the papers on the desk and make the planets in the mechanical model of the solar system on the windowsill rotate a little on their brass axes.

Change was definitely in the air.

He just hoped that, whoever and wherever this Ms Halliday was, she felt it too.

# CHAPTER THREE

SARAH woke with a start and sat up, her heart hammering.

Over the last few weeks she had got quite familiar with the sensation of waking up to a pillow wet with tears, but this was more than that. The duvet that she had kicked off was soaked and the cotton shirt she was sleeping in—one of the striped city shirts that Rupert had left at her flat—was damp against her skin. It was dark. Too dark. The glow of light from the landing had gone out and, blinking into the blackness, Sarah heard the sound of cascading water. It was raining.

Hard.

Inside.

A fat drop of water landed on her shoulder and ran down the front of her shirt. Jumping up from the low camp-bed, she groped for the light switch and flicked it. Nothing happened. It was too dark to see anything but instinctively she tilted her face up to try to look at the ceiling, and another drop of water hit her squarely between the eyes. She swore quietly and succinctly.

'Mummy,' Lottie murmured from the bed. 'I heard that. That's ten pence for the swear box.' Sarah heard the rustle of bedclothes as Lottie sat up, and then said in a small, uncertain voice, 'Mummy, everything is wet.'

Sarah made an effort to keep her own tone casual, as if water cascading through the ceiling in the middle of the night was something tedious but perfectly normal. 'The roof seems to be leaking. Come on. Let's find you some dry pyjamas and go and see what's happening.'

Holding Lottie's hand, Sarah felt her way out onto the landing and felt her way gingerly along the wall in what she hoped she was remembering correctly as the direction of the stairs.

'Please can we switch the light on?' Lottie's whisper had a distinct wobble. 'It's so dark. I don't like it.'

'The water must have made the lights go out. Don't worry, darling, it's nothing to be afraid of. I'm sure—'

At that moment loud shrieks from the direction of Angelica's room made it clear that she had just become aware of the crisis. Then the door burst open and there was a sudden and dramatic increase in the volume of her wailing. 'Oh, God—wake up, everyone! There's water *pouring* through the roof!'

Lottie's grip tightened on Sarah's hand as she picked up on the hysteria in her aunt's voice. 'We know,' said Sarah struggling to keep her irritation at bay. 'Let's just keep calm while we find out what's going on.'

But Angelica only did calm if it came expensively packaged in the context of a luxury spa. Fenella appeared beside her, ghostly in the gloom, and the two of them clung together, sobbing.

'Darlings, what on earth has happened?' As she joined them Martha's drawl was faintly indignant. 'I thought I'd fallen asleep in the bath by mistake. Everything's soaking.'

'Must be a problem with the roof,' Sarah said wearily. 'Mum, you look after Lottie. Angelica, where would I find a torch?'

'How should *I* know?' Angelica wailed. 'That's Hugh's department, not mine. Oh, God, why isn't he here? Or Daddy. They'd know what to do.'

'*I* know what to do,' said Sarah through gritted teeth as she made her way towards the stairs. Because that was what happened when you didn't have a man around to do everything for you; you developed something called *independence*. 'I'm going to find a torch and then I'm going to go out and see what's wrong with the roof.'

'Don't be silly—you can't possibly go climbing up onto the roof in this weather,' snapped Angelica.

'Darling, she's right,' said Martha. 'It's really not a good idea.'

'Well, let me know the minute you have a better one,' Sarah called back grimly. The dark house was filled with the ominous sound of trickling water and her feet splashed through puddles on the tiled floor of the kitchen as she searched for Hugh's expensive and unused collection of tools.

Amongst them was a small torch. Flicking it on, Sarah let its thin beam wander around the walls and felt her heart sink. Water was dripping from the ceiling and running down the walls in rivulets, just like the ones streaming down the window panes outside. The patio doors shed squares of opaque grey light over the wet floor. She opened them and stepped outside.

It was like walking into the shower fully clothed. Or maybe not quite *fully* clothed, she thought, glancing down at Rupert's striped shirt. Within seconds it was soaked and clinging to her, which at least meant that she couldn't get any wetter. Shaking her hair back from her face, blinking against the teeming rain, she sucked in a breath and forced herself to walk further out into the downpour, holding the torch up and pointing it in the direction of the roof.

The low pitch of the single-storey roof was easy to see, but the torch's weak light showed up nothing that would explain the disaster unfolding inside.

'Sarah—you're soaked! Darling, come in.' Her mother had appeared in the doorway, a raincoat over her elegant La Perla nightdress, an umbrella shielding her from the rain. 'We're way out of our depth here. Angelica and Fenella have taken Lottie with them to get help from the yummy man next door.'

Sarah directed the torchlight higher to the spine of the roof, squinting against the rain. 'But it's the middle of the night. You can't just appear on someone's doorstep at this hour.'

'Darling, we're damsels very much in distress,' Martha

yelled above the noise of the rain, collapsing the umbrella as she retreated indoors. 'This is an emergency. We can hardly wait until morning—we need to be rescued now.'

'Speak for yourself,' muttered Sarah disgustedly under her breath, dragging over one of the patio chairs so she could stand on it. Clamping the torch between her teeth, she used the drainpipe to hoist herself onto the low roof.

The tiles were rough beneath her bare knees, but they felt firm enough. Cautiously, shaking dripping hair from her eyes, she stood up, freeing her hands to hold the torch again. The roof sloped gently upwards to the main part of the house, and she carefully climbed higher, the dim beam of light wobbling erratically over the glistening terracotta tiles in front of her. They were uneven and bumpy but none seemed to be missing. Sarah directed the torch to the highest point, where the kitchen roof joined the wall. There seemed to be a gap…

At that moment she heard voices below and the wet blackness was suddenly flooded with blinding white light. Sarah gave a gasp of shock and, lifting her hands to shield her eyes from the glare, she accidentally let the torch slip from her grasp. She heard it clattering down the roof as she struggled to keep her balance on the slippery tiles.

'Bloody hell!'

'Stay there. Don't move.'

The light was shining right up at her, making it impossible to see anything beyond the silver streams of rain in its dazzling arc. Staggering backwards, she squinted into its beam, instinctively trying to see the owner of the deep, gravelly Italian voice while simultaneously peeling the soaking shirt from her wet thighs and bending her knees in an attempt to make it cover as much of her as possible.

'I said, keep still. Unless, of course, you want to kill yourself.'

'Right now I'm tempted,' Sarah muttered grimly, 'given that I'm half-naked and you're shining a spotlight on me. Could you possibly just turn that light off?'

'And if I do that, how are you going to see to get down from there?' He didn't have to raise his voice above the noise of the rain. It was rich and deep enough to need no projection.

'I was managing all right until you came.'

'Meaning you hadn't broken your neck yet. What the hell did you think you were doing, going up there in this weather?'

Sarah gave a snort of exasperation. 'God, you sound just like my mother. Can I just point out that I wouldn't be up here in any other kind of weather, since I'm trying to find out where the water's coming in. Up there I think I can see a—'

'On second thoughts, I don't really want to know,' he interrupted, and Sarah clearly heard the exasperation in his tone. 'I just want you to come very slowly towards the edge of the roof.'

'Are you mad?' She pushed dripping tendrils of hair back from her wet face. 'Why?'

'Because I know there'll be a joist there that will support your weight.'

'Oh, thanks a lot! Would this be a special steel-reinforced—?'

'Sarah, just do it.'

Hearing him say her name detonated a tiny explosion of shock in her abdomen that stopped her dead for a moment. Her mouth opened, though it was a couple of seconds before she was actually able to speak.

'How do I know I can trust you?' she said sulkily, squinting into the dazzling light, wishing she could see him. 'You could be anyone.'

'You don't, and I could, but now's not really the time for lengthy introductions. Let's just say that my name is Lorenzo, and right now I'm all that's standing between you and a very nasty fall.'

His voice was doing things to her. Inconvenient things, given her position. Irritation fizzed inside her. 'I don't mean to be rude when we've only just met, Lorenzo, but you're building your part up just a little bit. I'm not stupid, you know—I did check before I got up here that it was safe. The roof hardly slopes at all and the tiles are fixed down properly—'

Sarah took a step towards the edge and as she did so felt the tile beneath her foot crack and give way suddenly. She let out a sharp cry of anguish, her arms windmilling madly as she tried to keep her balance.

Suddenly she was afraid.

'It's OK. You're all right.'

'That's easy for you to say,' she gasped with a slightly wild laugh. 'You're not the one who's about to crash through the roof and end up on the kitchen table.' She closed her eyes for a second, waiting for the adrenaline that was pumping through her and making her feel shaky and unsteady to subside.

'That's not going to happen.'

'How do you know?'

'Because I'm not going to let it.' The beam of light swung away from her and she shivered in the sudden darkness. But a moment later he spoke again, and his voice was closer now.

'I can't do this and hold the torch, so you're going to have to listen very carefully and do what I say. OK?'

'OK.' Her voice sounded small and quiet. But perhaps it was just because her heart was suddenly beating very loudly, making the blood pound in her ears. The torch was on the ground far below, its powerful beam cutting through the indigo darkness and turning the rain on Angelica and Hugh's limestone patio into pools of mercury. Up here it seemed very dark.

'Come carefully towards the edge of the roof and stop when I tell you.'

Sarah did as he said, letting out another whimper of fear as she felt another tile crack. Rain was running down her face, making her eyes sting. She closed them.

'That's it. Stop there,' he ordered, and although his voice was harsh there was a peculiar intimacy to it. 'Now, reach out your arms. I'm going to lift you down.'

'No! You can't! I'm too heavy, I'll…'

But the rest of her protest was lost as she felt one arm circle her waist, and then she was being pulled against his body.

Through the thin layer of their wet clothes she could feel the warmth of his skin, his hard-muscled chest. Instinctively her hands found his shoulders, and even through her shock and fear she was aware of their power. Heat suddenly erupted inside her, tingling through her chilled body.

'Thank you,' she muttered, trying to pull quickly away from him as her feet made contact with something solid. Instantly the world tilted and her stomach gave a sickening lurch as she felt herself falling and realised she had just stepped off the edge of the table they were standing on. He grabbed her again, pulling her back into the safety of his arms.

'I'm beginning to think you have a death wish,' he said grimly, sweeping her legs from under her and holding her against him as he climbed down from the table in one fluid movement.

'If I did I could think of more elegant ways to end it all than falling off a roof while wearing nothing but my nightie. Now, *please,* put me *down.*'

'The gravel is sharp and you've got no shoes on.'

'I'm fine. I can manage. Please…' she said, miserably aware that by now his back was probably groaning with bearing the weight of her. Although he certainly showed no sign of noticing that she was heavier than your average feather pillow. Against her ear his breathing was perfectly slow and steady, and his pace easy. It didn't slow at all at her words either, she noticed with a thud of alarm and helpless excitement as they rounded the corner of the house and he made straight for the hulking shape of a large 4x4 that loomed out of the darkness. 'Where are you taking me, anyway?'

'Home.'

'Look, stop, please. And let me go!'

He sighed. 'If that's really what you want…'

Unreasonable disappointment shafted through her as he set her down on the wet gravel and stood back. She wobbled slightly as the sharp stones cut into her feet. Out of the warmth of his arms, she realised how cold she was.

'It is,' she said and hoped that the sudden feeling of uncertainty about that wasn't evident in her voice. 'Look, it's very kind of you to help, but we'll be fine here until morning. We've never even met before and there are five of us here, so—'

'Actually, you're wrong.'

'What do you mean?'

'Well, for a start, your family are already there, at Castellaccio.'

'What? But they can't…we can't…possibly descend on you. It's out of the question—we'll manage fine here.'

'Funny. That wasn't what your sister said. Or her friend—Fenella, was it?'

Bloody Fenella. Her words from earlier echoed mockingly around Sarah's head. *He sounds delish. I wouldn't mind getting on the right side of him…* Of course, never in a million years would she pass up the opportunity to get a foot in the door of a film director's luxury *palazzo*. Limping as quickly as she could after Lorenzo Cavalleri, it wasn't just the sharp gravel beneath Sarah's bare feet that made her wince.

He reached the car and pulled open the door. A small light inside went on and she felt her heart stop, and then start again with a painful thump as she caught a fleeting glimpse of hard cheekbone and sharp jawline darkened with stubble before he melted back into the darkness and went around to the other side of the car.

For a moment he had reminded her of the man in the pub that night. The man who had kissed her. But of course that was ridiculous; he was Italian, and male—that was where the coincidence ended. Getting into the car, she quickly did up her seat belt and, as he got into the driver's seat beside her, deliberately turned her head and looked out into the wet night.

She could hardly remember what he looked like anyway, she told herself crossly. Because it was unimportant. *He* was unimportant.

'First thing tomorrow I'll get a decent local builder to come and have a look at the roof and then hopefully we can get it sorted out,' she said stiffly as he started the engine.

'You know many decent local builders?'

'No, but I'm guessing that any local builder would be better than the idiots that Hugh and Angelica brought over from London. God knows what they've done.'

'My guess is they've put the tiles on upside down. Tuscan roof tiles curve slightly, and it appears they've laid them so that the water flows right down between the gaps. If I'm right the whole roof will need redoing.'

Sarah groaned. 'Oh, God, but the wedding's the day after tomorrow. I'll have to think of something.'

There was a slight pause, and then he said quietly, 'Why is it your responsibility?'

Sarah stared through the silvery lines of rain on the window. 'You've met Angelica and my mother. They're each as hopeless as the other, and we can't wait until Hugh and Guy get here if it's going to be sorted out before the wedding.'

'Hugh I've met, but who's Guy?'

The windscreen wipers beat a steady tattoo, like a heartbeat in the womb-like interior of the car, and warm air from the heater curled around her, making her chilled skin tingle. She felt suddenly very, very tired and leaned her head back against the soft leather seat, closing her eyes. 'Guy's my stepfather. Angelica's father. He's the kind of person who makes things happen and gets things done—especially for Angelica, but I suspect that re-roofing an entire house in under twenty-four hours is beyond even his capability.'

'You don't get on with him?'

'Oh, I do. You couldn't not. He's charming, witty, extremely generous…'

'But?'

She was dimly aware that the car had come to a standstill, but he didn't turn the engine off. Below the throb of the engine she could hear the rain pattering on the roof, and it made her feel oddly safe and protected. Or maybe it was this man that made her feel like that—this stranger, Lorenzo Cavalleri. For a moment she thought back to how it had felt to be in his arms when he had rescued her from the roof. The strength that she had sensed in him, that was more than just a matter of hard muscle…

She sat up abruptly and opened her eyes, feeling for the door handle.

*Rescued her.*

Uh-uh. She didn't need to be rescued. She didn't ask for it and she didn't want it. She could cope perfectly well without a man, and she wasn't going to make the mistake of letting her hormones rule her head again. Not after Rupert. Not after the man in The Rose and Crown that night. Perhaps she should ring Italian Accents Anonymous.

'He's not *my* father, that's all,' she said abruptly, pushing the door open and getting out of the car. The shock of the cold rain on her newly warmed skin was almost a relief.

Small world, thought Lorenzo, getting out of the car and walking round to where she waited by the *palazzo*'s double front doors. He felt a smile touch his mouth as he looked at her. She was standing perfectly still, perfectly straight, almost as if she was oblivious to the rain that was plastering her hair to her head and running down her face. Most women he knew would be horrified at the idea of being so thoroughly drenched—like her sister, for example, who had insisted on an umbrella being found before she would even make a dash for the car back at the farmhouse.

'The door's not locked. Please, go in.'

She didn't move. 'Look, I'm sorry about this,' she said as Lorenzo moved past her, pushing open the door. 'Really. It doesn't seem right. We don't even know you. Maybe we should just go and—'

The light from the hallway spilled out into the wet night. Standing back to let her go ahead of him, he saw her blink in the sudden brightness, and then watched her eyes widen, her lips part in silent shock as realisation hit her.

Her hand flew to her mouth, colour blooming in her rain-shiny cheeks as she took a couple of steps backwards into the darkness. Lorenzo reached out and grabbed her wrist, pulling her into the hallway.

'You're not going anywhere,' he said softly. 'Not this time.'

# CHAPTER FOUR

'THIS time.'

Pressing herself back against the closed door, oblivious to the grandeur of the enormous room in which she found herself, for a moment the only words Sarah's shocked brain could come up with were a numb echo of his. '*This time?* So you *knew?* All this time I've been out there making a complete and utter spectacle of myself, you knew it was me.' Horror crept over her as her mind replayed the events of the past hour in this new, humiliating light. 'You could have *said.*'

'And if I had?'

'I would have stayed up on the roof.'

She closed her eyes, hot shame flooding her as she thought about what she must have looked like from below in her skimpy shirt. How she must have *felt* when he'd lifted her down.

*Oh, God.*

Having to surrender your scantily clad self—all too-many stones of it—to the arms of a stranger was bad enough, but discovering that he wasn't entirely a stranger was infinitely worse. The man who had been shining a torch up her soaked-to-transparency shirt, the man who had lifted her considerable weight down from the roof, was the same man who had kissed her as a joke on her sister's hen night. It was almost more than she could bear.

'Exactly,' he said gravely.

At that moment they were interrupted by a familiar voice from the doorway. 'Oh, there you are, darling! Honestly, talk about drowned rat!' Sarah felt the colour deepen in her glowing cheeks as her mother advanced towards them, still in her nightdress and coat but now with a large drink in one hand, as if she were at a slightly bohemian cocktail party. 'Come through and get a towel, darling—we're all drying out in front of a lovely fire and warming up with some of Signor Cavalleri's excellent brandy.' She batted her eyelashes in Lorenzo's direction. 'He's been so kind, I can't tell you.'

Sarah gritted her teeth, feeling the way she had when she was at school and Martha and Guy used to turn up at her sports day in the open-topped Rolls-Royce, and loudly uncork bottles of vintage champagne while everyone else was opening flasks of tea. 'Mum, please,' she hissed, following her across the inlaid-marble floor and through a doorway on the right. 'I really don't think we can…'

She stopped. The room she found herself in had the same majestic proportions, the same ornate plaster panelling as the hall, but here the stately impact was lessened by the fact that it was incredibly untidy. Papers covered every surface, from the vast antique desk that stood between the windows, to the low table in front of the fire and the deep leather chesterfield sofa. Or the bits of it that weren't taken up with Angelica, Fenella, Lottie and a large grey dog.

'Lottie's fast asleep already, bless her,' Martha continued, peering down at her small pyjama-clad form. 'Isn't she sweet? Signor Cavalleri, I really must thank you for taking pity on us in our hour of need. Now we're all here, please let's introduce ourselves properly.'

Standing shivering in her wet shirt, Sarah gave a short, humourless laugh. 'I don't think there's any need for that. I believe that Angelica and Signor Cavalleri already know each other.'

Angelica blinked and shook back her silky blonde hair.

'Oh, no, I don't think so, but I believe you've met my

fiancé, Hugh? You were kind enough to come and offer your advice on—'

Beside her Fenella nudged her and murmured something inaudible, glancing at Sarah. Angelica's blue eyes widened. 'Oh, my goodness, yes! You were in the pub that night, weren't you? The Rose and Crown, on my hen night.'

Sarah felt as if there were something wrapped tightly around her neck as Lorenzo gave a curt nod.

'Oh, gosh—I don't believe it! What an *amazing* coincidence, isn't it, Fenella?'

'Amazing,' smirked Fenella, unfolding herself from the sofa in one elegant movement and letting the long cashmere cardigan she was wearing fall open to reveal little shorts and a vest top beneath it. 'Of course, if we'd had the chance to talk we might have discovered the coincidence sooner but, as I recall, Sarah rather naughtily monopolised you. You both disappeared rather suddenly too.'

Sarah snatched up a towel and began vigorously rubbing her hair, which was the only way she could stop herself from taking Fenella's elegant neck in her hands and wringing it. It also provided her with a diversion as she struggled to fit this new and unexpected information into the mental slot marked 'Bastard' she had created for the Screaming Orgasm man.

If Angelica and Fenella hadn't set him up that night, then why the hell had he kissed her?

From behind the towel she watched as he briefly shook the hand Fenella held out. 'As *I* recall,' he said casually, turning away, 'you were monopolising the rest of the males in the vicinity, so I'm sure it was no loss.'

'Well, how astonishing that you should find yourself in our very sleepy corner of darkest Oxfordshire,' Martha interjected hastily. 'I'm Martha, by the way. Martha Halliday.'

Lorenzo stopped, tensing into complete stillness for a second. Then he turned round again, his narrow eyes very dark.

'Not so sleepy, Signora *Halliday*.' Sarah noticed the slight emphasis he placed on her mother's surname. 'Certainly not on the night I was there. Have you lived there for long?'

'Since I was nineteen and I fell in love for the first time. You're right—it's nothing like it used to be,' Clearly eager to steer the conversation back into harmless waters, Martha was at her most chatty and expansive. 'I grew up in suburbia and it was like being dropped into the middle of a Thomas Hardy novel. Wildly romantic in theory, but the reality was harsh. In those days The Rose and Crown was a tiny little country inn where regulars used to help themselves from behind the bar and put the money in a box. Francis—that was my first husband—spent more of our married life in there than at home. He used to sit at a table in the corner by the inglenook and write. Said it was the only place he could keep warm enough to think in winter.'

'Write?'

'Yes. Poetry, mainly, but—'

'Mum,' Sarah hissed, 'it's three o'clock in the morning. I hardly think this is the time to be discussing literature.'

Especially not the singularly unsuccessful literary efforts of her father. Sarah just knew what Martha had been about to say next— that as well as endless volumes of strenuous, angry poems describing the industrialisation of the rural landscape, the late Francis Tate's canon also included a book, set in Oxfordshire and Tuscany. The fact that it too had been a complete commercial flop never stopped Martha from talking about it as if it were some work of staggering, underrated genius, much to Sarah's embarrassment.

'Sorry. Of course, darling, you're right,' Martha laughed, putting down her empty brandy glass. 'We've caused you quite enough disruption already, Signor Cavalleri. It's not too inconvenient to put us up for the night, I hope?'

'Not at all,' Lorenzo said tersely. 'Although I can't promise five-star service, I'm afraid. I should explain that I'm here alone at the moment. My housekeeper left a while ago and I haven't got round to finding a replacement yet, so you'll have to look after yourselves. You found the rooms all right?'

'Oh, yes, thank you.' Martha beamed. 'You have such a beautiful home, and perhaps tomorrow we can see it properly, but now, girls, I think it's time we took ourselves out of Signor Cavalleri's way.'

The dog lifted its head mournfully as Angelica and Fenella got up from the sofa and said their goodnights, but it didn't move. Sarah eyed it warily as she looked down at Lottie, wondering how best to pick her up without waking her. In the warm glow of the firelight she was curled up tightly, her hands tucked neatly beneath one rosy cheek, like a child in an old-fashioned picture book.

She jumped as a low voice broke the silence. 'So, you have a daughter.'

Her sudden indrawn breath made a little hiss in the quiet room. Lorenzo was standing on the other side of the sofa, watching her expressionlessly.

'Yes.' She wasn't as good as he was at keeping the emotion from her voice, and the short word bristled with defensiveness.

This was the point at which most men would say something bright and howlingly insincere about how sweet Lottie was, how adorable, whilst mentally calculating the quickest method of exit, but Lorenzo Cavalleri simply nodded. His eyes never left hers. It was as if he was looking right inside her. Sarah felt her stomach tighten with reluctant excitement as heat zigzagged down to her pelvis. And then she remembered that she was wearing nothing but a wet shirt, and that she'd towel-dried her hair so vigorously that she was probably doing a very good impression of Neanderthal woman. Quickly she bent over Lottie, hoping he wouldn't see that she was blushing.

'I'll help you get her to bed,' Lorenzo said flatly, and she was aware of him moving round the sofa to where she stood.

'No. It's fine. I can manage.'

'How did I know you were going to say that?' he said, his voice laced with sardonic mockery. 'Do you ever accept help?'

'I'm used to doing things myself, that's all,' Sarah muttered, wondering how she was going to bend down enough to gather Lottie up without completely exposing herself. Again. She wasn't sure if the fact he'd pretty much seen it all already made it worse or better. 'Lottie's father wasn't exactly the hands-on type.'

'Where is he now?'

'In bed with his ice-blonde, beautiful fiancée, I imagine,' she said bitterly.

Lorenzo nodded slowly. 'I see.'

She gave a harsh gust of laughter. 'I doubt it,' she snapped, sitting down abruptly on the sofa beside Lottie, bending forward to gather her into her arms from there.

They both jumped as the huge plasma screen above the fireplace flickered into life, displaying a close-up image of a woman's bare midriff—as smooth and brown and endless as a stretch of desert sand. The camera travelled upwards, lingering lovingly on the hollow between her incredibly firm, neat breasts, the ridges of her collarbones and the sharp jut of her jaw as she stretched her head back and opened her mouth in a breathless cry of pleasure…

Sarah's mouth dropped open too, although it was a look she couldn't carry off half as sexily as Tia de Luca.

Because there was no mistaking that was who it was. No mistaking those slanting eyes, as cool and green as apples, or the famous pillow-plump lips, which were now quivering with anticipation as the hero's mouth moved up the column of her throat towards them…

Sarah's sharp, high gasp matched Tia de Luca's as Lorenzo's hand slid beneath her thigh. The next moment the screen was black and empty again.

Whipping her head round, she looked at him. He was standing perfectly still, the remote control held in his hand. For a second Sarah glimpsed a blaze of some unidentifiable emotion in his eyes, but then it was gone; replaced once more by an expressionless mask.

He threw the remote control down onto the low table in front of the fire.

'You sat on it,' he said shortly.

Sarah stumbled to her feet. 'Oh, God, I'm so sorry.'

Lorenzo shrugged impatiently. 'No problem.'

She shook her head. 'No, not for sitting on the stupid remote. For saying that before, about you not knowing what it's like. To be left. I was forgetting. I mean, I don't know anything about it, but Angelica and Fenella were talking earlier about your wife and—'

'I'm sure you're tired,' he interrupted coldly. 'Perhaps I could show you to your room now.'

Sarah ducked her head, pushing back the trailing sleeves of her shirt as she prepared to pick Lottie up. 'Of course. Yes. Sorry.'

'Here. Let me take her. You're soaking.'

'So are you.'

'Yes, but I can take this off.' He was already undoing the buttons of his shirt, impatiently, with a kind of resignation that told her that he just wanted to get rid of her, with as little fuss as possible. And, of course, she didn't blame him. He must have been watching the film when Angelica interrupted him, asking for help. That explained why he was still awake, still dressed in the small hours of the morning...

It also explained the sadness she had sensed behind the mask. And probably it accounted for why he'd kissed her that night too, she thought with a wrenching sensation in her chest. When your heart was broken you'd do anything, use anyone to blot out the hurt and loneliness for a while.

Lorenzo didn't bother undoing all the buttons, pulling the shirt quickly over his head and throwing it hastily on top of the pile of books and papers on the table in front of the sofa.

'This way.'

Following him across the hallway and up the wide, sweeping staircase, she kept her eyes fixed determinedly on Lottie's head, resting against his upper arm. It was important not to allow herself to look at the wide shoulders or the way the muscles rippled beneath his olive skin, because then she might start making disloyal comparisons with Rupert's English pallor; his square, stocky frame that was showing the beginnings of a paunch.

There wasn't an ounce of spare flesh on Lorenzo Cavalleri. Sarah could see shadows between the ridges of his ribs, and his hip bones jutted above the top of his jeans. For all his strength, he was too thin, she thought with a twist of unexpected compassion.

'This is it.'

He stopped so suddenly in front of a closed door that Sarah, lost in forbidden thought, walked straight into him. Muttering apologies, she instantly leapt away. He opened the door and went into the room, but she stayed where she was in the dimly lit corridor, pressing herself against the wall and waiting for her breathing to steady. Looking around her, back along the corridor through which they'd just come, she realised guiltily that she hadn't taken in a single detail of her surroundings as she'd followed him through the *palazzo,* which was amazing considering that, from the little she could see now, it was pretty damned impressive.

Just not as impressive as Lorenzo Cavalleri's body.

She closed her eyes, tipping her head back against the panelling and trying to bring her wayward thoughts under control. Or her wayward hormones. It had been a long time since she and Rupert had—

'She's all yours.'

She opened her eyes, which was a bit of a mistake. He was standing in front of her, the low light from further along the passageway gleaming on the bare skin of his collarbone, the curve of his shoulder.

'Thanks,' she croaked ducking her head and sliding along the wall towards the bedroom doorway. 'For everything. And sorry.'

As she went into the bedroom she heard him say something in reply, but was so busy cursing her own gaucheness that she didn't catch what it was. Too late; through the half-open door she could hear his footsteps already dying away on the landing outside, and anyway a moment later all thoughts dissolved in her head as she turned to look around at the room.

It was as if she'd stepped into the pages of a book of fairy tales. The soft glow of the bedside lamp gleamed on the polished parquet floor and made the pale green silk curtains on the four-poster bed shimmer like waterfalls. Lottie lay against a froth of old white linen and lace like a miniature Sleeping Beauty, and Sarah gave a quiet sigh of delight as she imagined what her reaction would be when she woke and found herself in the midst of such storybook perfection.

The bed looked unbearably inviting, and all at once she realised that she was bone-tired and aching in every limb. She shivered, suddenly aware of the chill of the wet shirt against her skin, and longing to be between the soft, dry sheets. Quickly she lifted the shirt over her head and was just pulling the heavy covers back when there was a soft knock at the door behind her.

Her heart practically jumped right out of her chest. Gasping, 'Wait a second!' she dived beneath the covers and pulled them right up to her chin, the second before the door opened wider and Lorenzo's shape appeared in it.

He advanced towards the bed. The lamplight cast inky shadows in the hollows of his cheeks and accentuated the deep lines etched around his mouth and between his brows, making him look very, very tired. And sad. For a second an image of the woman on the screen flickered into Sarah's mind.

'I thought you might want this, but I can see you're managing perfectly well without.'

Tentatively Sarah inched herself upwards in the bed, clutching the sheets against her as she cautiously extended an arm to take what he held out to her. It was a T-shirt. A grey T-shirt, soft and faded.

'Thanks,' she said, not meeting his eye.

She expected him to turn and leave straight away, but he didn't. The room was very quiet, very still. The only sound was the distant rattle of rain on the windows and the gentle sigh of Lottie's breathing.

'So…' he said gruffly, lifting one hand and pushing his hair back from his forehead and then letting it fall again. 'You still haven't introduced yourself properly.'

'I don't need to. You already know my name.'

'Do I?'

Something about the way he said it made her heart lurch and her gaze fly up to meet his. 'Sarah,' she said, almost warily. 'My name is Sarah. You said it when I was on the roof.'

He nodded slowly, his eyes still boring into hers with an intensity that made her shiver and burn. '*Si*. But that doesn't mean I know who you are.'

'Then we're equal,' she said ruefully, looking down. The T-shirt he'd just given her was twisted into a knot between her hands. 'Apart from the fact that I'm nobody, and apparently you're some world-famous film director.'

'I'm hardly world-famous,' he said dismissively. 'And you're not nobody.'

'Yes I am.' She laughed uneasily, and beside her in the bed Lottie stirred and sighed, turning over so that she was lying on her back, her chestnut curls falling over her face, until she pushed them impatiently away with one plump hand. For a few long moments neither of them spoke or moved as they waited for her to settle again. Watching her face, the little frown that flickered across it for a second, the way her rosebud mouth pursed and then relaxed into a dimpled smile, Sarah found that she was smiling too. When she spoke her voice was very soft.

'I'm a mother. That's it. That's all that matters, anyway.'

She looked up, and the smile died on her lips when she saw the shuttered, cold expression on Lorenzo Cavalleri's face. He turned away, walking across the miles of gleaming parquet to the door.

'It's very late. I'm keeping you up.'

'Many would argue that it was the other way round,' Sarah said hastily. 'Look, I'm really sorry for the intrusion. My family is a full-on nightmare. You'll seriously regret your kindness, believe me.'

He stopped at the door and turned back to look at her for a second with a brief smile of distant courtesy. 'Not at all,' he said tonelessly. And then he was gone, shutting the door very quietly behind him.

*Not at all.*

Sarah Halliday couldn't begin to know how wrong she was. As Lorenzo walked away down the corridor he felt edgy with adrenaline, almost unable to take it in.

Oh, yes, it was a small world, and it was being managed by a very benevolent God. Lorenzo sent up a silent prayer of thanks to Him for delivering Francis Tate's stubborn and elusive daughter right into his hands.

It was more than he could ever have hoped for. Now the rest was up to him.

# CHAPTER FIVE

SARAH propped the broom up against the wall and looked round despondently. Almost an hour of hard labour in the water-logged wreck of the farmhouse kitchen had resulted in minimal improvement. She'd been able to sweep out the worst of the water and make a start on wiping down the surfaces, but there was nothing at all she could do about the plaster coming away from the walls or the ominously sagging ceiling.

An hour of hard labour hadn't quite succeeded in shifting the restless, jumpy feeling she had somewhere deep down inside of her either. It had been there all night, and had made sleep elusive and unrefreshing, filled with uneasy dreams in which Lorenzo Cavalleri had held her against his bare chest and carried her along endless dark corridors…

With a sigh of exasperation she seized a cloth from the sink and began to scrub vigorously at the grimy marble worktops, as if by doing so she could also scour the unwelcome feelings from her mind and her body. It was because she was missing Rupert, she told herself fiercely. He might not have been great at a lot of things, like taking Lottie to the park, and mentioning that he was intending to marry someone else, but he'd certainly found the time to call round regularly for swift, no-nonsense sex.

She was ashamed to admit how much she missed it.

Sexual frustration, that was what all this was about, she

thought, scrubbing hard. What she was feeling was a normal, healthy part of the process of letting go. She'd been with Rupert a long time, so it was inevitable that she would go through lots of stages of grieving. Fantasising about other men was obviously one of them. Breathing hard with exertion, she paused to peel a soggy copy of a celebrity magazine from the countertop where Angelica had left it. She was just about to deposit it into the bin when a headline on the cover caught her eye:

'BITTERSWEET BABY JOY FOR TIA DE LUCA.'

Sarah stopped dead, the magazine dangling between her fingers, suspended above the bin. Then, glancing guiltily around, she dropped it back down onto the bit of worktop she'd just cleaned and began to flick through. The pages were damp and stuck together, but she eventually located the full-page picture of Tia de Luca languishing on a pile of fuchsia-pink silk cushions wearing a chiffon kaftan-type thing that managed to make her look simultaneously demure and maternal without compromising her high-octane sex appeal. Propping her elbows on the worktop, Sarah began to read.

'Oh, yuk…' she muttered, skimming increasingly quickly over the interviewer's gushing inventory of Tia's finer points. *'Miss de Luca's legendary beauty has a delicate, luminescent quality that is even more powerful in the flesh than it is on the big screen. Her figure is impossibly slender…'* Sarah gave a grimace of irritation *'…showing only the barest hint of the pregnancy she announced last week. At the mention of this her extraordinary eyes cloud for a moment. "I've wanted a child for so long, and I thought my husband felt the same way," she whispers, referring, of course, to acclaimed director Lorenzo Cavalleri, whom she has just divorced after five years of marriage. "He found it impossible to adjust to the idea of a child in his life, but I'm so lucky that Ricardo shares the joy I feel about this blessed miracle…"'*

'Hard at work, I see,' said a mocking voice behind her.

Sarah whirled around. Grabbing the magazine, she clasped

it behind her back with shaking hands as she looked into Lorenzo Cavalleri's coal-black eyes. He was unshaven, and the sparklingly bright morning light highlighted streaks of grey in his hair that she hadn't noticed before. Her heart gave an uneven kick.

'I was… I mean, I am… I'm just…'

He shrugged, a tiny smile lifting the corners of his sad mouth. 'I'm teasing. When I left your sister was having a leisurely breakfast, so I shouldn't feel too guilty about taking a break from clearing up her house.'

'Was Lottie there?' Sarah asked automatically, then instantly wished she hadn't. From what Tia de Luca had said, this man didn't even want his own child around, never mind someone else's. Behind her, the magazine seemed to be burning her fingers.

'Very much so,' he said drily. 'She seems to approve of Castellaccio.'

Sarah winced. 'Oh, dear. I'm sorry. Where we live there's barely enough room to swing a hamster, and she's already wildly overexcited about the wedding and being a bridesmaid and everything.' Hurriedly she turned and dropped the magazine into the bin before picking up the cloth and scrubbing at the worktop with great focus. 'I'll just finish cleaning up in here and then I'll…'

She stopped. He had come to stand right beside her, and now reached out to cover her hand with his, stilling it. 'What? Clean the rest of the house and retile the roof before lunch?'

She froze. Common sense told her to pull her hand from beneath his and put as much distance between them as possible so he didn't notice that she was blushing like a schoolgirl and breathing like an asthmatic who'd just run a marathon. But she didn't want to. It felt too good. 'Well, maybe not quite,' she said in a low voice, 'but at least I can make it look a bit better for the wedding.'

He made a little sound of contemptuous disbelief, and moved his hand, stepping back and pushing it through his hair. '*Dio,* Sarah…'

She started cleaning again, covering the worktop in sweeping strokes that she hoped would make her look brisk and efficient. 'I know it's still a mess in here, but Angelica doesn't even have a mop. Once I get the right equipment it'll all be much easier, and then I can—'

'I didn't mean that,' he said curtly. 'Why is this your problem? It's your sister's house. Your sister's wedding.'

'Ah, yes, but, since I'm doing the catering, it's pretty much my problem, because until I can get this place cleared up I can't even make a start, and I'm going to be cutting it pretty fine as it is.'

Lorenzo shook his head in disbelief. 'Wait a minute. You're doing what?'

'The food.'

His face darkened. 'For the whole wedding? *Dio*. How many people are coming?'

'Only thirty.' He didn't have to be so appalled at the idea of her being in charge of the food, she thought sulkily, going over to the sink and holding the cloth under the tap. 'It's just a small, simple ceremony for close friends and family. They're having a big party in London next month.'

'Couldn't they get professional caterers?'

She turned off the tap and squeezed the cloth. Hard. 'I *am* a professional caterer. I worked for a company doing business lunches in the city.'

Those dark, narrow eyes didn't miss a thing. 'Worked? You don't any more?'

She looked around for more worktop to clean. 'No. No. I—er—left after an incident involving a cake at an engagement party.' She laughed uncertainly. 'Some girls wear engagement rings. I wear engagement cakes. It wasn't pretty. Anyway,' she said hurriedly, 'money's been a bit tight since then, so instead of buying a wedding present I offered to do the food. I really must get a move on—I still have to shop for ingredients.'

'Get some shoes on,' he said grimly. 'You're coming with me.'

She shook her head. 'Oh, no, I can't. I couldn't put you to any more trouble, and besides, there's no point in shopping for food until I've cleaned up here. There's nowhere to put anything.'

'We're not going shopping—yet—and you're not cleaning up here. I'm taking you back to Castellaccio.'

She opened her mouth to argue, as he knew she would, but he didn't wait to hear what she was going to say. Levering himself upright, he stalked across the kitchen to the door, saying, 'The kitchen there isn't perfect, but at least it's unlikely to give thirty of your sister's closest family and friends serious food poisoning.'

Direct hit, he thought with satisfaction, hearing her footsteps following him across the gravel a moment later. He barely knew her, but instinct told him that, though she'd fight like a cat to maintain her own spiky independence, she had an inbuilt selflessness that wouldn't allow her to put her principles before other people's well-being.

'OK. You win. Again. I'll come back with you. But first, can I go and get a change of clothes for me and Lottie? I won't be a minute.'

She was standing in the sunlight, and with her hair scraped back in some sort of pink, glittery band, wearing denim shorts and the too-big T-shirt he'd lent her, she looked oddly vulnerable.

'Of course. I'll wait in the car.'

He'd expected to be waiting for ages, but it seemed that she'd hardly gone before she was back again. She'd swapped the grey T-shirt for a coral-pink linen shirt that brought a glow to her clear skin. Skin that was, he noticed wryly as she opened the car door and got into the passenger seat, still completely bare of any trace of make-up.

'Sorry to keep you waiting,' she said breathlessly, throwing a battered straw basket stuffed with clothes into the space by her feet. In her hand she carried a pair of child's red canvas pumps which she laid on her knee, and in that second Lorenzo was pierced by an image, as clear as if he'd shot it himself on

35 mm film, of Lottie's small bare feet as he'd slid her into bed and folded the covers over her last night.

He averted his eyes.

'You didn't.' His voice sounded colder and harder than he'd intended. 'In my experience when a woman goes to change it involves at least five outfits and takes about an hour.'

'I don't have five outfits, which I suppose makes things a lot simpler.' The 4x4 bounced over a pothole in the road and she steadied herself, shifting her position at the same time as he moved down a gear so that his hand brushed her warm bare thigh. She jerked away again as sharply as if she'd touched a live wire.

For a moment neither of them spoke, then she said in a brave, bright voice, 'Anyway, this is really kind of you. At least if I can prepare the food in your kitchen, then tomorrow morning I'll come and get it and—'

'Don't you ever stop fighting?' he said grimly, turning into the driveway and accelerating slightly up the avenue of trees. Palazzo Castellaccio stood at the end; square, uncompromising and unadorned, its only concession to any kind of ornament being the *limonaia* on the side.

'Fighting what?'

He stopped the car in the shade at the side of the house and turned off the engine. The sudden silence seemed to crackle with tension.

'Logic. Reason. Common sense,' he said quietly. 'The farmhouse is a mess, and not even you can put it right in time for tomorrow. I didn't just mean that you could cook here—I meant that the wedding would be held here too.'

She laughed shakily, pulling at a trailing bit of straw that was unravelling from her basket. 'No. No way. It's impossible. Please, don't even think about mentioning that to Angelica because before you know it your house will be completely overrun with the whole bridal steamroller and you'll wish you'd never set eyes on any of us.'

He couldn't help smiling at that. 'I don't think so.'

'Y-you're sure?' Hesitantly she looked up. Straight into his eyes. And he knew that he had her exactly where he wanted her. Sarah Halliday was a girl with an outsized sense of responsibility, and he knew that after he'd done her family a favour on this scale she'd find it hard to say no to anything.

Including film rights to her father's book.

# CHAPTER SIX

'MUMMEEEEEE!'

Sarah was making lists at the table at one end of the cavernous kitchen when Lottie came hurtling in through the open doors to the courtyard. Sarah put her pencil down and caught the wriggling little body that hurled itself at her.

'There you are, sweetheart. I was wondering where you'd got to. Auntie Angelica said that you and Granny had gone exploring.'

'Yes—we found the church where Auntie Angelica's getting married, and met the gardener—he's called Alfredo—and there's a temple thing with steps up to it. And we saw a statue of a man with no clothes on and you can see his—'

'Good old Granny,' Sarah interrupted firmly, kissing the top of Lottie's head and setting her down again. 'Trust her to give you the full, x-rated, unabridged tour.'

'You must come and see it. Granny said you should. And Granny said it's not rude because it's *culture.*'

'I see, so Granny thinks I don't have enough culture in my life, does she?' Sarah said crossly.

'No,' said Martha drily, coming in from the bright sunlight outside. 'Granny thinks you don't have enough naked men in your life. Mind you, you could probably do better than that one. *Not* very impressive. I'm sure you wouldn't have to look very far to find a much more virile specimen, if you haven't already…' Her blue eyes twinkled wickedly. 'Ah, hello, Signor Cavalleri! We were just talking about you—weren't we, Sarah?'

'Were we?' Sarah snapped, feeling heat explode in her cheeks as she frowned down at her list with what she hoped was an air of total preoccupation. God, why did her mother have to be so embarrassing? Lorenzo Cavalleri had been married to someone widely acknowledged as the most beautiful woman in the world. As if he was going to be interested in flirting with her.

'No, you weren't, Granny,' Lottie protested. 'You were talking about the statue we saw in the garden of the man with no clothes on. You said that he had—'

Martha laughed, completely uncontrite. 'OK, my darling, I think you've got me into quite enough trouble already!' She turned her dazzling smile on Lorenzo. 'I was just about to say how very, very kind you are to be doing this for us. Really. It's so much more than anyone could have expected, and I can't begin to tell you how grateful we are—now, that *is* true, isn't it, Lottie?'

'Yes.' Lottie nodded vigorously, her eyes widening with sincerity. 'We think this might actually be the most beautiful place in the whole world. Auntie Angelica is very lucky to have her wedding here, and I'm very lucky to be a bridesmaid here, but you're luckiest of all because you live here.'

Lorenzo nodded. 'I'll remember that.'

Lottie looked at him thoughtfully for a moment. 'Do you live here by yourself?'

A faint smile touched the corners of his mouth. 'Yes.'

'It's very big for one person.' Lottie's voice held a slight air of disapproval and Sarah noticed anxiously that she was looking at Lorenzo with that beady, appraising look that suggested more devastatingly to-the-point questions and observations might follow.

Lorenzo met her gaze unflinchingly. 'It is,' he said gravely. 'Far too big. It has sixteen bedrooms.'

Lottie's eyes were as round as saucers. '*Sixteen?*' she echoed. 'But that's—'

'Enough,' Sarah interrupted firmly, and then, seeing Lottie was about to protest, added, 'And don't argue.' She softened her words with a swift kiss on the head, then picked up her list. 'Right, I'd better get going. Do you want to come with me, sweetheart?'

Lottie frowned. 'Where are you going?'

'Shopping.' Looking round, Sarah picked up her straw basket and busied herself checking that her purse was in it. 'To buy food for Auntie Angelica's wedding.'

'I'd rather stay here, with Granny.' Lottie hesitated, then added kindly, 'But I don't mind coming with you if you'll be lonely on your own.'

'How about if I go?' Lorenzo was looking at Lottie, his expression completely neutral. Giving a happy little jump, Lottie clapped her hands and cried 'Yes!' at exactly the same moment as Sarah said an emphatic

'No.'

'You might get lost,' said Lottie pityingly. She smiled at Lorenzo. 'I think you should definitely go too. Mummy's always saying she needs a nice man to take her out.'

After yesterday's rain it seemed hotter than ever, the sky a hard, glittering arc of polished lapis lazuli.

Lorenzo had dropped her off in a little street that ran down to the main square, and stepping out of the climate-controlled interior of the car had felt like walking into an oven. But in many ways it felt easier to breathe in the scorching heat than it had done when she was near him in the air-conditioned car.

The market was set out in the piazza, the brightly coloured awnings of the stalls contrasting vividly with the stinging yellow and rich, earthy reds of the buildings all around the square. The sun was relentless, but it seemed a shame to dim the astonishing colours behind dark glasses, so Sarah slid them up onto her head and enjoyed the vibrant glare. Wandering through the crowds of people, her list clasped in her hand, she had quickly become completely absorbed in her task, pausing beside stalls piled high with produce to pick up a tomato and test the firmness of its flesh, or hold a melon to her nose, inhaling its cool green perfume.

The colours, the scents and textures dazed her. She was in Italy. *Italy.* All around her she could hear the most beautiful language on earth rising and falling in musical cadences, the occasional isolated word resonating in her head and striking chords of half-forgotten meaning. She was here. Far, far away from London and traffic jams and office blocks, in the spiritual home of good food, great art and hot sex.

The thought took her by surprise and made her heart perform a little acrobatic flip.

Her Italian was basic, but the stallholders were so friendly that she soon found that much could be achieved with a smile and a gesture. Slivers of velvety prosciutto were pressed on her—salty-sharp and melt-in-the-mouth; smoky Provolone cheese; olives that tasted of sunshine and Italy. She bought bags of peppery fresh rocket, courgettes with the flowers still attached, lemons as big as tennis balls and heads of fragrant garlic from a stout, smiling man in a striped apron, whose eyes twinkled above his bristling moustache as he heaped her purchases into her basket and pressed a ripe peach into her hand once she'd paid.

'*Grazie, signor.*'

He dismissed her thanks with a wave of his plump hand and, dark eyes snapping, answered with a stream of rapid Italian that went completely over her head. Biting into the peach, Sarah shrugged helplessly and laughed. 'I don't understand!'

'He's saying that it's a pleasure to serve such a beautiful girl who clearly understands good food,' said a low voice behind her.

Sarah didn't turn, but felt the laughter fade on her lips. Her mouth was filled with the exquisite sweetness of the peach and her stomach tightened.

The stallholder's smile widened into a beam of delighted

recognition when he saw Lorenzo, and he broke into a flood of excited conversation that involved much arm-waving and laughter. Taking another bite of the peach, Sarah stepped to one side, so that she wasn't caught in the middle of all the exuberant back-slapping as the man greeted him as an old friend. The stallholder's infectious bonhomie was in direct contrast with Lorenzo's habitual aloofness, but somehow that only served to emphasise the gorgeous richness of Lorenzo's deep, grave voice. Eating her peach in the sunshine, she listened to him with a pleasure that was almost physical.

*Actually, there was no almost about it.*

Suddenly she gave a start, as she realised that both men were looking at her, as well as a fair number of passers-by, who had temporarily stopped passing by and were lingering, feigning interest in piles of oranges while stealing curious glances at her and at Lorenzo. Oh, God, did she have peach juice running down her chin? Hastily she wiped her mouth on the back of her hand. Lorenzo was smiling at something the man had said, shaking his head, but his eyes met hers and she felt a bolt of electricity shoot through her, like the lightning before a sudden summer storm.

'An old friend?' she asked when they eventually made their escape in a flurry of handshaking and *ciao*s.

They were walking across the square, away from the market. Lorenzo was carrying a box containing the courgettes, on top of which a handful of dark, bulbous truffles had mysteriously been added.

'No. But having a job that gets your picture in the papers makes people feel that they know you.'

Sarah looked down at her feet in their battered flip-flops. Her toes bore the chipped remains of some pale green nail varnish Lottie had got in a party bag ages ago. 'What did he say?'

Lorenzo shot her a speculative, sideways glance. 'He asked if you were the new woman in my life.'

Sarah took her glasses from the top of her head and pushed

them on again, so she didn't have to meet his eye. 'Oh, God. How embarrassing for you. I'm so sorry.'

'Don't be. When I said no, he asked why not.' He began to weave through the busy tables of a little restaurant in a sunny corner of the square.

Surprised, she asked, 'Where are we going?'

'For lunch.'

She stopped dead, feeling deeply foolish. 'Oh. Right. OK, then…you should have said. I'll just look round the shops and I'll meet you when you're finished—'

Shifting the box of courgettes to under one arm, he put his other hand in the small of her back and drew her gently, firmly forwards into the dim interior of the restaurant.

'No, you won't. You'll have lunch with me. After all, you have to eat.'

Inside the restaurant was empty, cave-dark, the colour of its walls impossible to make out behind the forest of framed photographs, newspaper cuttings, old menus and napkins scrawled with the indecipherable signatures that covered them. Lorenzo led her to a table in the farthest corner and pulled out a chair for her.

'Not really. I'm hardly going to fade away, am I?' she muttered, picking up the menu and holding it in front of her face so he couldn't see her flaming cheeks. 'As the man said, I clearly know all about good food.'

Gently he removed the menu from her hands and put it down on the table. And then he reached across and pulled off her sunglasses.

'It was a compliment,' he said, very quietly.

His dark gaze enveloped her. It was like standing outside on the warmest summer night, and feeling perfectly safe in the blackness. For a moment she just looked back at him, not thinking, not wanting to think. Only wanting to feel that indefinable, inexplicable sense of being protected…

She blinked, and looked away with a quick, self-deprecating smile.

'Of course, this is Italy. I'd forgotten how different it is from buttoned-up, poker-faced England,' she said soberly, pushing her chair back and getting to her feet. 'Excuse me a moment.'

In the tiny ladies' cloakroom out the back, with the scent of garlic wafting in from the kitchen, Sarah looked dismally at her reflection in the mirror. Her face was shiny and the sun had already brought out the freckles across her nose, but that was nothing compared to the disaster that was her hair. With a groan of dismay she tugged it free from the Disney princess band that had been the first thing that came to hand this morning and frantically tried to pull her fingers through the wild curls that last night's soaking followed by enthusiastic towel-drying had turned into a tangled mane.

She exhaled heavily so that one curl fluttered upwards for a moment before bouncing back onto her nose. So, the question was, which was worst? The pink, glittery hairband with its picture of Cinderella's disembodied head, or the mad hippy look? Grimly, she turned on the tap and ran her hands beneath the blissfully cool water before smoothing them over her hair in an attempt to flatten it into some semblance of normality. At least with it down she would have something to hide behind.

Back at the table, Lorenzo poured dark red wine into two glasses and watched her make her way through the tables towards him. That was something at least, he thought wryly. It wouldn't have surprised him if she'd made a run for it through the kitchens.

He was used to women clinging. Fawning. Playing complicated games that were calculated to catch his attention and keep him interested, which he suspected was exactly what Tia's last fling had started out as. But this girl, he thought, looking at her as she smoothed a hand over the curls she'd just let down, this girl would obviously rather be pretty much anywhere else, and she couldn't hide it if her life depended on it.

That was one of the first things he'd noticed about her, back in England. Her emotions were written all over her sweet, open face, which should make it a hell of a lot easier for him to find out more about her father, he thought idly. He just had to get her to relax enough to open up a bit.

He pushed a glass towards her as she sat down again, and was rewarded with a quick smile that brought out the dimples in her smooth cheeks and made her look about sixteen.

'Oh, God, I really shouldn't. I've got to cook this afternoon, and I haven't even decided on the menu yet. Lunchtime drinking is a really bad idea.'

'You haven't decided on the menu? *Bene,* in that case we can call this research.'

She looked at him warily, but he was absurdly pleased when she took a large mouthful of wine. 'Research?'

He nodded to the swarthy man nonchalantly polishing glasses in the shadows behind the bar. Gennaro was far too discreet to approach them without invitation, but he came forward now with a wide smile.

'Sarah, I'd like you to meet Gennaro, owner of this place, and consummate menu-planner.'

She smiled—a warm, genuine smile—half rising from her chair as she held out her hand. Gennaro took it, but leaned forward and kissed her on both cheeks too, and when he turned back to Lorenzo his dark eyes gleamed with approval.

'*Delizioso,*' he said in rapid, local Italian. 'Your taste in women is definitely improving.'

Lorenzo pulled out a chair and motioned for him to sit down. '*Non e come cio,*' he said curtly. It's not like that.

'*Che?*' Sitting down, Gennaro threw his hands up in mock despair, replying in impenetrable dialect, 'This is the first woman you bring here in seventeen years who doesn't look like she's going to order an undressed chef's salad and spend the whole time picking out the pancetta, and you tell me *it's not like that?*' He shook his head hopelessly.

Very deliberately Lorenzo switched back to English. 'Sarah's a cook,' he said, hoping that Gennaro would pick up the warning note in his voice. 'It's your advice about *food* I'm after, *grazie mille.*'

Gennaro laughed. 'Of course. My pleasure. It is my second favourite subject. How can I help?'

'You can start by bringing us some of your bresaola, and then whatever you're recommending today to follow.'

'Ah—you came on the right day, my friend. Today we have porcetta slow-roasted with herbs. *Fantastico.* Leave it to me. I bring you the best food in Tuscany, Sarah.'

'Bresaola,' Sarah repeated as Gennaro disappeared in the direction of the kitchen. She took another mouthful of wine and Lorenzo noticed that her expressive dark eyes were shining with a light he hadn't seen in them before. 'That's beef, right?'

He nodded. 'Air-dried and salted, like prosciutto, but forget any preconceptions you have about what it's like until you've tried Gennaro's. It comes from a local farmer, whose identity Gennaro keeps top secret. However,' he drawled with a lazy smile, 'I'm absolutely certain that *you* could charm him into spilling the information.'

She laughed awkwardly, looking down and realigning her knife and fork on the scarred pine table top. 'Is there a shortage of women around here or something?'

'No. What makes you say that?'

'It's just that I don't usually have men falling over themselves to do things for me.'

'Maybe that's because you usually give the impression that you'd rather die than accept help. Or kill anyone who offers it.'

'I would not,' she protested hotly, 'I—'

She stopped as Gennaro reappeared with several plates. Sensing the atmosphere, he slid them quickly onto the table with a murmured 'Buono appetito' and melted away again.

Her eyes were troubled as they briefly met his across the table. 'Sorry. You're right. I'm not good at accepting help, but I hope you don't think it's because I'm ungrateful.'

'I don't.' He picked up a piece of warm bread and dipped it

into the shallow dish of oil, then tore off a strip of the dark, silken bresaola and held it out to her. 'But I'd like to know what it is.'

She took the bread from him and, slightly self-consciously, took a bite. He watched, fascinated, as her expression changed, a slight frown of concentration appearing on her smooth forehead.

Frustration mixed with amusement as he realised she was totally focused on the food and his question was now forgotten.

'Good?'

She nodded vigorously, so that her curls bounced. She swept them back with an impatient hand. 'Better than good. Unbelievable.' She tore off another ribbon, crumbling some delicate shavings of parmesan over it with quick, light fingers. 'And it would be perfect as a starter for the wedding—beautifully simple to prepare, although the cost might mean it's out of the question.' She'd almost been talking to herself, he realised, but then suddenly she glanced up at him and smiled guiltily. 'What a fabulous place. D'you come here a lot?'

He hesitated a fraction too long before answering. 'Not as much as before.'

Not now he was alone, he meant. Tia had liked to eat out, although eating really didn't come into it. She'd liked to be seen and photographed, and she particularly liked to be seen and photographed looking as if it were the last thing she'd expected. Gennaro's, with its atmosphere of unpretentious authenticity, made her look grounded and low-maintenance, which was laughably far from the truth.

Sarah nodded, looking away quickly as she understood his meaning. 'Oh, look,' she said in surprise. 'That's you, isn't it? In the picture?'

Wiping her hands on her shorts, she got up from the table and went to look more closely at the photograph, which hung on the wall just to his right, amongst all Gennaro's other bits of memorabilia and souvenirs left by previous guests. He glanced quickly to see which picture she had noticed, and saw that it was of him and Tia at one of the tables outside, a bottle of Prosecco in an ice bucket between them. It had been during a break from filming, and Tia was spilling out of a low-cut lace-up bodice. Aware of the camera on her, she was throwing her head back and laughing while he looked at her, unsmiling.

'Gosh.' Sarah's husky voice was wistful. 'She's so beautiful.'

'Yes.' He sounded unnaturally harsh, and he realised it must seem as if it bothered him to be reminded of her. He dragged a hand through his hair and tried to make up for it by adding, 'It was taken last summer when we did some location work here for a film. That's why she's wearing that dress.'

'Oh, yes. I didn't even notice.' Sarah gave a breathy little laugh as she came to sit down again. 'That's how cool I am—for all I know film stars dress like that all the time. What film was it?'

'It's called *Circling the Sun.*'

'Should I have seen it? I can never get a babysitter, so I'm terribly behind everyone else when it comes to cinema.'

He poured more wine into both their glasses. 'It's not out yet. It'll be premiered at the Venice Film Festival at the end of the month.'

'And your…Tia…is the female lead?'

'Yes.' He picked up his glass and took a mouthful of wine. 'Alongside her new partner, who played the title role.'

His tone was bland, completely without bitterness, but even so, Sarah felt her throat tighten with compassion. What she'd felt that day in the boardroom of Lawson Blake as she watched Rupert holding hands with the blonde in the business suit paled into insignificance next to how it must have been for Lorenzo, directing their love scenes, watching reality overlap fantasy, life obliterate art.

Squashing the last few crumbs of bread beneath the ball of her thumb, she desperately cast around for a subtle way to divert the subject on to safer ground. 'What's the film about?'

His wide, down-turned mouth twitched into a momentary grimace. 'Galileo, supposedly.'

'He invented the telescope, didn't he?' She leaned back,

flashing a quick smile of appreciation up at Gennaro, who appeared to take their empty plates and melted away again with a wink.

'Amongst other things.' Lorenzo dragged a hand over his face. In the dim light of the restaurant he looked much older than the man in the photograph watching his laughing wife. He leaned forward, resting his arm on the table, his dark gaze steady on hers. 'Galileo was a fascinating man, who challenged everything that people had previously believed about the universe. He was also a devout Roman Catholic who had a passionate relationship with a woman called Maria Gamba and fathered three illegitimate children with her.' He gave an ironic smile. 'It's that aspect of his life that the American backers wanted to emphasise, rather than his revolutionary theories on the solar system.'

Gennaro was weaving through the tables towards them, a huge white plate in each hand from which fragrant clouds of steam were rising. Part of the skill of the successful restaurateur lay in knowing when to talk to your guests and when to leave them alone, and Gennaro was a very successful restaurateur. Putting the succulent porcetta before them on the table, he silently left again without breaking the fragile spell of intimacy that had come to rest over the small table.

'Lottie won't approve,' Sarah said, breathing in the aroma of herb-spiked porcetta and suppressing a moan of greed as she picked up her fork. 'She's obsessed with the solar system, but not so much with passionate relationships.'

'She's a bright little girl.'

'Yes.' Sarah finished her delicious mouthful and took a sip of wine before adding, 'I think she must get that from her father. And the lack of interest in relationships.'

'What's he like?'

'Clever…analytical,' she said thoughtfully. 'Focused, ambitious, driven…' She laughed. 'When I say all that it makes me realise how amazing it is that we ever got together in the first place.'

'How did you meet?'

He wasn't eating much, she noticed, instantly feeling embarrassed that her own plate was already half-empty. She laid down her fork and played idly with a rocket leaf, twirling it between her fingers. 'He worked for an investment bank in the city. I often did business lunches for them, and I guess that maybe at that stage he thought I'd make a good corporate wife.'

'Love at first sight?' His voice was gently ironic, but his steady gaze held no trace of amusement. Sarah felt herself squirm a little beneath such scrutiny, aware of the warmth that was stealing up through her. Helpless to stop it.

'Pregnancy on first night,' she said in a low, self-mocking voice, trailing her finger through the rich juice on her plate and sucking it. 'Poor Rupert. He must have felt the noose tightening around his neck. It was all such a far cry from what he wanted, but—'

Lorenzo gave a little snort of disdain. 'What *he* wanted? What about what you wanted?'

'Oh, I just want Lottie to be happy,' she said quickly, with what she hoped was an air of finality. She was talking too much about herself. To a top film director whose address book was no doubt stuffed with the names of fascinating, beautiful people. She was bound to have a certain novelty value for him, but she didn't want to push it too far. 'To have a good life, and grow up well-adjusted and able to look after herself. She already does a pretty good job of looking after me, so I probably shouldn't worry.'

Smiling, she leaned back and pushed her plate away in a gesture that was supposed to stop herself from eating every remaining scrap and probably picking the plate up and licking it too, and also give him a chance to change the subject. But his dark, focused gaze didn't falter.

'What about before that,' he said quietly. 'Before you were a mother. What about *you?*'

She paused. 'Funnily enough, I wanted to come to Italy. To

live here, and learn all about Italian food. But anyway, it's irrelevant now. I *am* a mother.' She laughed, trying to lighten the atmosphere a little. 'Not a very good one, admittedly.'

And suddenly, unaccountably she felt the needle-sharp sting of tears at the backs of her eyes. Biting her lip, she looked away, towards the door of the restaurant and the bright, sunlit square beyond, blinking as everything in her fought desperately not to humiliate herself again by crying in public for no good reason whatsoever.

She'd shredded the rocket leaf now, so that only the stalk remained. Very gently he took it from between her fingers and Sarah gave a sharp little inward breath as he took her hand in his.

'Why do you do that?'

'What?' she whispered.

'Put yourself down all the time.'

She sniffed and gave a watery smile, not meeting his eye. 'Sorry.'

'And apologise for everything.' He sighed wearily. 'I work in an industry where everyone devotes their whole lives to making themselves look significantly better than they really are—in every way—and yet you do the opposite. Why is that?'

The warmth and strength of his hand on hers was doing strange things to her ability to think clearly. Her throat still prickled with unshed tears, but stronger than that was the sudden insistent pull of desire low down in her pelvis.

She closed her eyes for a second, shaking her head. Fighting it. 'I don't know. Guilt, probably.'

'What do you have to feel guilty about?'

Her laugh was edged with despair. 'Where do I start? For not giving Lottie holidays in Disneyworld or Mauritius. For not having those pink shiny nails with the white tips that other mothers have. For not being able to make her father love me enough to stay around for her, for not giving her brothers and sisters…'

For the briefest second his hand tightened reflexively on hers. 'She wants brothers and sisters?' he said flatly.

'She's never said that, but I know the rest of my family think she's missing out. And I do think that she should spend more time with children and less with adults. She's such a funny little thing, an old head on young shoulders...'

Sarah stopped mid-sentence. Across the table their hands were still entwined, but his face wore an oddly blank expression, and she suddenly realised that it was she who was holding his hand now, squeezing it hard as she spoke about worries she was used to keeping locked safely inside. Flaming embarrassment swept through her as she realised how tedious this must be for him. Held hostage by an emotionally unstable single mother intent on using him as a therapist.

Swallowing hard, she carried on in a rush, disentangling her fingers from his as she made an attempt at laughter. 'Which can't be my influence because I have the head of a particularly gormless teenager on the shoulders of a middle-aged housewife.'

He didn't smile. When he spoke his voice was stiff and rusty. 'What about you? Do you want more children?'

She shook her head, the laughter dying on her lips. 'I love her so much. And it's not that I don't think I'd love another child, because I'm sure that kind of mother-love is infinite, but...'

'Go on.' He might not still be holding her hand, but his gaze was so intense that it felt almost as if he were. It enfolded her, drawing out the truth that she hadn't dared to admit to anyone before.

'It hurts too,' she whispered. 'The worry, about whether I'm doing the right thing for her, the anxiety about whether she's happy or not. The...*responsibility*. I couldn't do it again. I don't want to. Does that make me an awful person?'

He smiled now, and it was filled with a mixture of compassion and pain and strength that made her feel shivery inside. 'No,' he said gently. 'Not at all.'

# CHAPTER SEVEN

As THE car bumped up the track back to the *palazzo* Lorenzo cast a surreptitious glance at Sarah in the passenger seat beside him. Her face was turned away as she stared out of the window, so all he could see was the afternoon sunlight glinting on the coppery highlights in her hair, her hands clasped round a bag of groceries on her lap.

Her knuckles were white.

He wasn't sure what had happened back there in the restaurant. He'd been making progress, getting her to open up, so why the hell had he allowed himself to get sidetracked by asking her about children, for pity's sake? He was supposed to be focusing on her father, on *her*, not himself.

And it was going to be hard enough getting to know her without complicating matters with his own issues. He felt the ghost of a smile touch his lips as he remembered the way her face had lit up as she ate, the passion she clearly felt for food which she was at such pains to hide. Gradually, millimetre by cautious millimetre, she had relaxed a little, allowed herself to talk. But it seemed that every time he got close to her she pulled back. Clammed up.

He suppressed a sigh of frustration.

She reminded him of Lupo. Lorenzo had come across him in the backstreets of Pisa when he'd been filming there, and the dog had been so badly beaten that, even though he was starving, he was too mistrustful of humans to come and take food from him. They'd been on location for three weeks, and it had taken Lorenzo almost that long to get close enough to touch him.

He still remembered the sense of achievement it had given him.

As they passed through the arched gateway to the *palazzo* she turned back towards him and gave him a small, shy smile.

'Thanks for today,' she said softly. 'For helping me get all the food, and for organising Gennaro's mystery farmer to deliver the other stuff. I don't know what I would have done without you.' She paused, her lips twitching into one of her swift, wicked smiles. 'Frozen pizza, probably.'

'Your sister and her friend don't look like they eat much,' he remarked drily. 'You might have got away with it.'

She laughed—and it was so unexpected and so good that it made him smile too. He pulled the car around the side of the house, and in the distance they could see people sitting on the lawn, and Lottie running across the grass, Lupo lolloping at her heels.

'Oh. Hugh's arrived. And Guy,' said Sarah, and her voice was suddenly flat and cold.

'Darling, that was marvellous, as always. A triumph. How can tomorrow's food beat that?'

'Oh, Guy, you're very kind.' Sarah leaned across her step-father to take his empty plate. 'It was only a very simple risotto. I hope tomorrow's food is a little bit more memorable.'

'How's the kitchen? D'you have everything you need?'

She shrugged slightly, the cheap polyester lining of her dress rustling as she moved around the table in the candlelight. 'It's amazing. Gorgeous, just like the rest of this place.'

They were eating at a long table in the *limonaia,* the candles in their ornate wrought-iron candelabra reflected in the rows of windows now that the summer night had deepened to indigo. Leaning back in his chair, Hugh smiled fondly across at his wife-to-be. 'I must admit it's all worked out rather well. When you rang and told me about the roof my heart sank, but you've done jolly well to sort all this out. Well done, darling.'

Gritting her teeth, Sarah kept piling up the plates.

'Oh, it was nothing really,' Angelica said airily. 'From what you'd said about Signor Cavalleri—Lorenzo—I thought he might be difficult, but in fact he couldn't have been kinder. Although there aren't many men who can resist Fen when she's in persuasive mode.'

Fenella smirked. 'I did ask him to join us for dinner, but he said he had work to do. Shame.'

Sarah picked up the salad bowl and balanced it awkwardly on top of the teetering pile of crockery. She didn't blame Lorenzo for shutting himself away in his study instead of joining them for dinner. She would have given just about anything to do the same, or to go up and join Lottie in between the cool linen sheets of the fairy-tale bed, but she still had a lot of preparation to do for tomorrow, so that luxury was a long way off. Crossing the courtyard on her way back to the kitchen, she took a deep breath of warm, herb-scented night air and consciously tried to loosen the iron band of tension that seemed to be gripping her head.

Why did her family always do this to her? It was bad enough when it was just her mother and Angelica, but their scatty helplessness was simply irritating. Guy and Hugh were another thing altogether. They'd only been there a few hours and already they'd taken over, striding through Lorenzo's home with an arrogant complacency that suggested that they'd planned the whole thing. As always, Sarah instantly felt like the hired help.

What must Lorenzo feel like? she wondered with a stab of anguish. This was his home. It seemed profoundly wrong that he should be forced to retreat to his study while her loud, insensitive family took breathtaking advantage of his courtesy. His kindness.

And he was kind, she thought with a stab of surprise, setting down the pile of dishes on the mammoth butcher's block in the centre of the kitchen. A sudden shiver shimmered through her whole body as she thought back to lunch in the little restaurant, the way he'd made her feel as if he was interested in her. As if she was important.

*Desirable, almost...*

Which was ridiculous. He'd been married to Tia de Luca, for pity's sake. He was a world expert on *desirable,* and she didn't even make it into the qualifying round.

Sighing, she dried her hands and pushed back her tangled curls. It was important not to make the mistake of mixing up courtesy with genuine interest. He had an inherent integrity and a natural honour that clearly dictated that he look out for people. Especially people like her.

She wondered who looked out for him, now his wife had gone. He seemed so strong, so in control, but from the emotion she had glimpsed in his eyes, the lines etched into his angular face, the ridges of his ribs on his powerful, too-thin body, she suspected this was an illusion.

She expelled a shaky breath. Better not to think about his body.

Her eyes fell on the huge pan of risotto standing on the stove, and she levered herself away from the sink with a renewed sense of purpose, grabbing a clean bowl. He'd been so sweet to her today, the least she could do was try to repay that a little.

The hallway was in half-darkness as she walked through it on bare feet, a tray in her hands, but she could hear the faint strains of music coming from behind the closed door of Lorenzo's study, floating languidly through the warm violet night. She caught a glimpse of herself in an ornate Venetian mirror as she passed; the steam of the kitchen and the humidity of the evening had made her hair wilder than ever, and her eyes in the half-light were shadowed with exhaustion. She hesitated for a fraction of a second, wondering whether to abandon the tray with the pasta and the wine and rush upstairs to hastily slap on some make-up, but quickly dismissed the idea, smiling a little at her own foolishness.

It would take more than a bit of under-eye concealer to put her in the same league as Angelica and Fenella and Tia de Luca. Major cosmetic surgery and liposuction wouldn't even do it.

She paused at the study door, listening. It was a dreamy orchestral piece, an arrangement of soaring strings, melancholy and beautiful, and, leaning against the doorframe in the majesty of the shadowy *palazzo,* she felt her throat tighten with an unexpected rush of emotion. Oh, dear, she had to pull herself together. With the tray in her hands she couldn't even blow her nose. Or knock, she realised, making a clumsy attempt at it with one elbow.

The door flew open and the wine sloshed over the rim of the glass as she staggered forward into the room.

Lorenzo was sitting amid the chaos at his desk, papers spread out all around him. He looked up as she made her undignified entrance, and for a second she saw surprise and then anger flash across his face, before it resumed its deadpan expression.

'Sorry, I just thought—'

With a swift, savage jab of a remote control he silenced the music, and Sarah's voice sounded loud and unnatural in the sudden silence.

'—you should eat.' She hesitated, moderating her tone so she wasn't shouting like a madwoman. 'I tried to knock, but I couldn't,' she added lamely, holding up the tray by way of explanation.

But he wasn't even looking at her. There was a sinister, focused energy to his movements as he gathered up the papers around him, shoving them into an open drawer and shutting the book that lay open before him as she approached the desk.

'You didn't have to do this,' he said tersely, and his tone told her what he was too courteous to say in words. That he wished she hadn't.

'It was no trouble. Obviously. I mean, I'd cooked for *them,* anyway, so…' She put the tray down on the edge of the desk. The dog pushed against her knees, looking up at her longingly as he caught the scent of food. At least someone appreciated the gesture, she thought miserably. 'Sorry about the wine. I'll get some more in a—'

'No.'

The word was like a gunshot in the quiet room. There was a small, shocked silence, before Sarah turned and all but ran to the door. She had just reached it when Lorenzo spoke again, making a deliberate and very obvious effort to soften his tone. 'Thank you for this.' He gestured to the bowl of cooling risotto. 'It looks superb.'

Muttering a meaningless reply, Sarah closed the door and fled back to the kitchen.

*Cazzo.*

Lorenzo dropped his head into his hands and exhaled heavily, cursing again in the sudden, thick silence. He couldn't have handled that more appallingly if he'd tried.

Lupo, alarmed by the swearing, slunk off and lay down in front of the empty fireplace. Lorenzo reached over and switched on the music again, more quietly this time, then opened the desk drawer where he had hastily shoved the location photographs and Francis Tate's book.

Instead of hiding them, maybe he should just have told her. Asked her. Whatever. Come clean, anyway.

But it was too soon, and he was scared of frightening her off. He wasn't sure why she'd refused permission before, but he understood that if he was to have any chance of making this film he was going to have to win Sarah Halliday's trust, and that meant getting to know her. Trying to understand her and what made her tick. From what he knew of her already he realised that could be a very long, very delicate process.

Especially if he behaved like that.

Picking up the half-full glass of wine from the tray, he slumped back in the chair. No, it was too soon to say anything to her yet. Not only did he need to understand what it was that made her refuse his first offer, but he also wanted to make sure that when he asked her again he could present her with a proposal that would do justice to his vision, and to her father's work. A proposal that she couldn't turn down.

He'd do whatever it took.

And he'd better start with an apology.

*Don't think about it. Just concentrate on making the custard. At least that's something you can do right...*

The thoughts circling Sarah's head kept time with the rhythm of her spoon as she stirred the pale-primrose mixture of egg yolks and cream in the pan. Consciously she made an effort to slow the rhythm, which had increased from steady and soothing to fast and furious as her thoughts strayed again to what had just happened.

The look on his face; a mixture of anger and impatience that he hadn't been able to hide fast enough.

*Don't think about it. Keep stirring. Slow. Calm.*

She gave a sigh of despair, blowing the damp hair off her forehead as she did so. Over the years her love of cooking may have had a very detrimental effect on her hip measurement, but it had certainly saved her sanity on several occasions, and this was definitely one of them.

God, it was hot. Everyone else had gone to bed long ago, extinguishing the candles in the *limonaia* so that the open doors of the brightly lit kitchen had been a lone beacon of welcome for every moth and mosquito in the area. They had launched bombing raids on the light above the table, dropping, stunned, into the vinaigrette dressing she had made to accompany the bresaola and the cream she had whipped for the cake, until eventually it seemed simpler to just close the doors and swelter.

And swelter she did. During the day the castle-thick walls of the *palazzo*'s amazing kitchen kept the space cool, but now, with the oven on and not a breath of air from outside, the heat gathered and swelled within them. Sarah's hair was damp with sweat as she kept her stove-top vigil over the custard, and beneath her apron the nylon lining of her dress stuck to her body like a polythene bag.

Another boiling surge of shame rose inside her as she remembered the way Lorenzo had looked at her when she had walked into his study, with that mixture of irritation and alarm. With a groan she pulled desperately at the apron strings knotted around her waist. Yanking the apron over her head, she wiped her damp face with it, making sure that her stirring didn't falter. It was cooler without it, but not much. Her dress was clinging to her like bindweed, so that it was impossible to breathe. She couldn't bear it any longer. Undoing the small pearl button at the neck, she dropped the spoon long enough to pull the dress down over her shoulders and let it fall to the floor.

The relief was blissful.

Instantly she felt calmer, more in control. She picked up the apron and looped it back over her head, loving the feel of the sweat cooling on her back as she tied it round her again. If anyone came in she would still look perfectly respectable from the front, but the likelihood of that happening was remote. It was almost two o'clock in the morning; everyone was asleep. Silence lay over Castellaccio's lovely rooms like a sepia shroud, a brief spell of peace before the frantic activity of the wedding tomorrow.

The wedding. She felt overwhelmed with weariness at the thought.

Earlier she'd heard Lorenzo pointing Guy in the direction of the cellars, where the tables that had been used at his own wedding were stored, and her heart ached for him as she realised how awful it must be to have all this taking place around him. No wonder he had looked at her with such annoyance. She wondered if he'd been thinking about Tia; if that beautiful, poignant music held some special significance for them both.

The mixture in the pan was thickening now, approaching that magical point where its transformation to the rich, unctuous crème patisserie that was needed for traditional Italian wedding cake would be complete. Sarah kept stirring, not taking her eyes off it for fear of missing the crucial moment when it would go too far and curdle; not wanting to lose her nerve and take it off the heat too soon.

The door opened.

Stupidly, for a second all she felt was a distant irritation at being disturbed at such a critical time. And then, of course, she looked up and saw it was Lorenzo, bringing back the tray, and remembered at that exact moment that she had taken her dress off.

Horror drenched her; a suffocating wave.

She half turned, so that she was standing at an awkward angle beside the cooker, facing him stiffly. The huge butcher's block stood between them, affording her a measure of protection.

'Just leave the tray on there,' she said quickly.

He put it down.

'*Grazie*. It was delicious.'

His tone was distant and formal, and she replied with the same stiffness. 'No problem. As I said, it was no trouble, but I'm sorry to have disturbed you.'

He hesitated for a moment, then sighed. 'No, I came to apologise to you. For being so rude. I'm very antisocial when I'm working.'

Sarah glanced down and let out a yelp of dismay, yanking the pan off the heat as she realised—too late—that the glossy, silken crème of a moment ago was now separating into a disastrous grainy mess.

'What's the matter?'

'The custard's curdled,' she moaned, gritting her teeth against the tide of vitriolic curses that would virtually bankrupt her if Lottie had been in earshot. Lorenzo was by her side in an instant, silencing her anguished protests as he removed the heavy pan from her hands, leaving her free to rush to the sink and turn on the cold tap.

Water cascaded down so forcefully that it sprayed all over her, but she hardly noticed. Spinning round to get the pan, she almost collided with him bringing it over to her, and for a split second they hesitated, staring helplessly at each other. Suddenly the heavy air seemed to pulse with meaning. His eyes burned into her as she reached out to take the pan from him, her hands closing over his on the handle.

He let go immediately, standing back as she plunged the pan into the cold water, then as she bent over the sink and started to whisk for all she was worth he leaned over and held it steady for her, his eyes never leaving hers.

Except when they moved downwards, to where her breasts were virtually falling out of her bra beneath the apron.

She gave a low moan, trying to focus her attention on what she was doing. What she was *actually* doing, not what she wanted to do, and what every atom and fibre of her being was screaming at her to do. *Like twist her body round so that she was standing in front of him, lift her arms and wrap them around his strong, tanned neck, tilt her face up and press her lips against his hard, set mouth...*

Oh, God, it was no good. The custard was disintegrating, and so was she. Falling apart. Desperately she redoubled her efforts, whimpering with the effort of not giving up. Or giving in.

'Sarah...stop.'

Lorenzo barely recognised that guttural rasp as his own voice. Letting go of the pan, he took hold of her upper arms, wrenching her round. He could feel the heat coming off her damp, voluptuous body and as he touched her she gave a shivery gasp, jerking beneath his cold, wet hands.

That was what did it, what tore through his iron self-control. That shiver of sensual awareness seemed to reverberate through his own body and galvanise him into actions he couldn't control. Suddenly he was pulling her against him as their mouths met and their lips parted and he was running his slippery hands over her bare back, beneath her hot, vanilla-scented hair and dripping cold water on her burning skin.

The kiss was hungry, devouring, urgent. She moved round so that she was leaning with her back against the sink, her fingers grasping his shoulders as their teeth clashed. Lorenzo could feel the jut of her hip bones against his, rising, pressing against his thudding body. His arousal was so sudden, so intense it was almost painful. He fumbled for the bow at the back of her apron, stretched to breaking point as his fingers moved across her bare, satin-smooth back. He wanted to have her, now, standing up against the sink…

As if she'd read his mind she shifted slightly, tearing her lips from his for a moment as she hoisted herself upwards so that she was half sitting on the edge of the worktop. The movement made a little space between them, and without the bewitching ecstasy of her mouth on his, her hot body pressed against him, Lorenzo was pierced through with sudden, chilling awareness.

*What the hell was he doing?*

He took a step backwards, thrusting both hands into his hair, balling his fists and pressing them against his temples.

'No,' he rasped. '*No*. This is wrong.'

He'd come in here to apologise, *per l'amore Dio*. He was supposed to be winning her trust, not stripping her of her self-respect. And that was exactly what he'd do to her if he took her now, like this, for a few moments of snatched pleasure.

He turned away, not wanting to see the expression on her flushed, lovely face change from wanton arousal to disbelief and then aching hurt. Wanting to give her that bit of dignity at least. And wanting to explain that he was doing it for her own good, because he knew that she was too sweet, too giving and generous, too vulnerable to use like that.

But he didn't.

'Forgive me,' he said harshly, and he left the room without looking back.

# CHAPTER EIGHT

'MUMMY. Wake up. It's *today*.'

Lottie's loud stage whisper in Sarah's ear and the feel of her soft palm against her cheek broke into Sarah's dreamless sleep. She half opened her eyes with a moan.

It felt as if she'd only just got to sleep. When she'd eventually slipped beneath the single linen sheet beside Lottie last night she'd lain there for hours, staring into the hot darkness as regret and self-recrimination buzzed around her head and thwarted desire pulsed through her tense body. It was amazing that she'd slept at all.

She rolled over, pulling the pillow over her head and squeezing her eyes shut against the bright slice of sunlight falling through a gap in the curtains. However, Lottie was not to be diverted.

'Did you make a new cake? Does it have little people on the top that look like Auntie Angelica and Uncle Hugh? Can I put on my bridesmaid dress now?'

'Lottie, you're like an alarm clock,' Sarah groaned from under the pillow. The cake was the last thing she wanted to discuss, so in an effort to distract her she groped for Lottie's nose. 'Do you not have an "off" button?'

Lottie laughed delightedly. 'I do, but you're not allowed to use it because you have to get up. The big hand is on the twelve, and the little hand is on the *nine*.'

Instantly Sarah sat bolt-upright, throwing the pillow down

and clutching her head as Lottie handed her her watch. 'See?' she said helpfully. 'Nine is definitely past get-up time, isn't it? So can I put on my bridesmaid dress now?'

Panic joined the misery and self-pity weighing down Sarah's heart. The wedding was at eleven.

'No. You can very quickly have breakfast in your pyjamas and put your dress on afterwards,' she muttered, staggering out of bed and clumsily pulling on yesterday's denim shorts and coral-coloured shirt, which were lying on the floor where she'd dropped them, before her life had taken another unerring swerve towards disaster.

Downstairs, the kitchen that she had cleaned up in a trance-like frenzy last night before she'd finally fallen into bed now looked as though Genghis Khan and five hundred of his hungry marauders had just passed through it. Sarah followed the sound of voices from the courtyard and found an impromptu break-fast party in full swing, complete with champagne and a whole lot of people she'd never laid eyes on before. Hugh's old school friends and city colleagues, she guessed, judging by their con-fident, drawling voices and the casual arrogance with which they'd taken over the place.

'Mummy, why didn't you let me put my dress on?' Lottie hissed, tugging urgently at her hand. 'Everyone else is dressed properly. It's *embarrassing.*'

She was right. There was no sign of Angelica, of course, but Hugh was already in his morning-suit trousers and white shirt, his very English complexion still slightly pink from the shower. She was nearly knocked sideways by the cloud of expensive aftershave that hung around him as he came over to press a glass of champagne into her hand.

She took it numbly.

'We were wondering when you were going to surface, old thing,' he said heartily. 'Had to dig around to find breakfast our-selves, but not to worry, we managed OK in the end.'

Sarah forced a smile of sorts. 'What a relief. You are clever.'

The irony in her tone was completely lost on him. Taking a hefty slug of champagne, he pulled over one of the newcomers, another city type who was already perspiring in his morning suit. 'Jeremy, this is Sarah, Angelica's sister, who I was telling you about.' A tiny flicker of surprise and pleasure briefly illuminated the frozen darkness inside Sarah's head, but it instantly died again when Hugh continued, 'Remember? She's the one in charge of the food, so it's her you have to sweet-talk about your wedding present.' He winked mischievously at Sarah.

Her heart sank even further. Jeremy beamed, rocking back on his heels and looking very pleased with himself.

'Oysters,' he boomed. 'A hundred and twenty of the blighters, fresh from the good old English Channel. Angelica's favourite—a big surprise for her. Thought they'd make a super starter for the wedding breakfast.'

Hugh clapped him on the back fondly. 'You sly old devil, that's damned fantastic. Isn't it, Sarah?'

Frankly, 'damned fantastic' was not exactly how Sarah would have described the careless havoc wreaked on her menu. She was still grappling for a more appropriate choice of words for Jeremy and his unexpected wedding gift as she looked despairingly down into the crate of oysters an hour later. Still dressed in yesterday's clothes, her hair still uncombed and her teeth unbrushed, she had spent the morning clearing up the kitchen—again—as well as charging round overseeing some of Hugh's more biddable friends setting up tables in the *limonaia* and positioning the vast arrangements of stephanotis and white roses delivered by the florist. And there was still the small problem of the cake to sort out.

Sucking in what was meant to be a calming breath, she was assaulted by an eye-watering smell of seaweed from inside the crate and instead felt another surge of fury, resentment and despair. Dropping the lid hastily back on the box and its unpromising-looking contents, she swore with satisfying unrepentance. Twice.

'What's it worth not to tell the swearing police?'

She stiffened instantly as she glanced up and saw that Lorenzo was standing in the doorway to the courtyard.

'How long have you been there?' she said, wishing she could sound as cool and nonchalant as he did.

'Long enough to know you're not having a good day.' He didn't move. 'Shouldn't you be getting ready for the wedding?'

'It looks like I won't make it down to the church.' She turned away, picking up a pile of side plates and moving them pointlessly to a different place on the worktop.

'Why not?'

She nodded to the crates. 'Oysters,' she said, unable to entirely keep the bitterness from creeping into her tone. 'A surprise addition to today's menu from Hugh's best man. Unfortunately I haven't the faintest idea what to do with them, but I imagine whatever it is will take a couple of hours at least.'

He came forward then, slowly. Sarah's skin tingled all over with embarrassment and wicked, shameful longing as her body recalled last night. She couldn't bring herself to look at him, but his voice was as devoid of emotion as ever. 'What about the cake?'

She couldn't breathe. When she tried to speak it sounded as if she was being strangled.

'Disaster.' Which pretty much summed up everything else too. 'The custard was too far gone and—'

He cut her off, cold and decisive. '*Tutto bene.* Leave it to me. I'll arrange a replacement from Gennaro. No one need ever know.'

'No,' she said unhappily. No one needed ever know what had happened, or why. Not that they'd believe it anyway. 'Thanks.'

He nodded, and for a second he seemed to hesitate, as if he wanted to say something and wasn't sure where to start. Then he sighed. 'Where's Lottie?'

'Upstairs. My mother's getting her ready.' Sarah's voice cracked, and blindly she picked up the side plates again. Suddenly that, on top of everything else, was almost more than she could bear. Totally unused to expensive clothes and smart shoes, Lottie had been beyond excited about the pale gold silk dress with its froth of tulle petticoats that had hung, shrouded in crackling plastic, on the back of Sarah's bedroom door for the last couple of months. She'd been counting the days until she'd be wearing it for real, and the thought that right now she was upstairs, squirming with excitement as somebody else buttoned her into it was so...

Unfair.

*Hell-o?* She sneered silently at herself. *Since when had life been fair?*

'Go up and find her,' Lorenzo said curtly, taking the plates from her. His fingers brushed hers and she jumped back, shaking her head with unnecessary vehemence.

'No. It's fine. My mother will have it covered, I'm sure.'

'Then go up and get yourself ready.'

'No, really, I can't.' She glanced at her watch and gave a suicidal smile. 'They'll be leaving for the church in half an hour, and even if you take care of the cake I really do have to work out what to do with the sodding oysters. Open them for a start, I suppose.'

'No.' Firmly, he took hold of her shoulders and turned her round so that she was facing the door. Sarah felt her insides leap with treacherous joy, and she had to tense herself against it, holding herself very, very straight and stiff as he propelled her gently forward and opened the door for her. His voice in her ear was husky and grave. 'Leave it to me. Oysters should never be opened until they're ready to be eaten. Unless you want to give everybody food poisoning.'

She knew when she was beaten.

'Not quite *everybody*,' she muttered darkly, ducking her head and hurrying towards the stairs.

*'Ciao, Gennaro. E grazie mille...'*

Lorenzo put down the phone and sighed heavily, rubbing his hands over his face. Problem solved: thanks to Gennaro, he'd secured a suitably impressive wedding cake and arranged to borrow a kitchen assistant and two of his waiting staff. They would be arriving at the *palazzo* within the hour.

It would cost him, of course. But at twice—no, ten times the price it would only be a fraction of what he deserved to pay.

Of course, her stepfather should be paying too, he thought bitterly, getting up and walking stiffly to the window. Hugh and his friends were out there, adjusting their ties, posing for photographs around a shiny red Ferrari that had appeared in front of the house, white ribbons fluttering across its bonnet. Anger hardened in Lorenzo's chest. Vulgar cars like that didn't come cheap, but then money clearly wasn't a problem for either Guy Halliday or Hugh Soames.

They were the ones who should be reaching into their Savile Row pockets to pay for cakes and catering staff, but of course there was no chance that was going to happen while they had Sarah to do everything for them for nothing. The sunlit morning blackened in front of his eyes as he thought of last night, when she had still been slaving away while everyone else was asleep—relaxed with wine and replete after the dinner she had cooked for them earlier. It had been almost two in the morning when he had come across her in the kitchen: pink-cheeked, exhausted, shiny with sweat. He recalled the heat and the panic he had felt coming from her body...

He slammed his fist down on the windowsill with such force that Lupo yelped and cowered. Guilt instantly assailed him.

More guilt. To add to the burden of remorse that, after last night's incident in the kitchen, lay across his shoulders like a mantle of lead.

To her idle, selfish family Sarah was nothing more than a pair of hands to cook them excellent meals and to clear away afterwards, invisibly and efficiently. He had watched them. He had watched *her, per l'amore di Dio*. No one concerned themselves with her as a person—how she felt, what she wanted. And the awful thing was that he had almost done the same.

Treated her as a warm, voluptuous body. A ripe pair of lips...

Self-disgust hardened inside him. He barely knew Sarah Halliday, but he'd spent enough time with her to understand that the last thing she needed was empty, meaningless sex. No matter how fleetingly pleasurable. Her self-esteem was low enough already without being used in that way.

No. If he wanted to gain her trust and get her to open up to him, it wouldn't be by seducing her.

Unfortunately.

The roar of the Ferrari's engine outside and whoops and cheers from the bridegroom's party cut through his thoughts. Which was probably just as well. He sighed, and was just about to sit down at his desk again when he heard voices in the hallway.

Angelica must be coming down. He glanced at his watch. It was barely twenty minutes since he'd sent Sarah upstairs to have a shower and get ready; surely she couldn't have managed it in that time? Which meant she'd be missing out on seeing Lottie in her finery.

Grabbing the small camera he kept for location research, Lorenzo crossed quickly to the door and opened it a little. Angelica was coming slowly down the stairs, the sunlight shimmering on her papery silk pearl-white dress, the gossamer-light froth of her veil. She was smiling for the photographer who was waiting below, his shutter clicking like a machine gun. There was something almost triumphant in her bearing, and the expression on her face was one of utter serenity and self-assurance.

Behind her Fenella was wearing a dress of dull gold that clung to her body; no doubt chosen to show how thin she was. He ignored her, focusing his camera on the little girl who bobbed in their wake, her eyes wide with solemnity and awe beneath her crown of ivory roses.

His chest constricted suddenly. He should have been ready for it by now, but the pain still took him by surprise sometimes, closing around his throat so tightly it felt as if he were being strangled.

He zoomed in on Lottie's face, keeping his eyes fixed on the viewfinder. The camera was his shield. It distanced him from life and all its complications and difficulties. Like Galileo's telescope, it enabled him to see things that he couldn't bear to examine without its impassive filter. On the small screen he watched Lottie let go of her posy of roses with one hand and push a stray curl back from her face. As she did so her dark eyes flickered upwards and she gave a smile which lit up her face and carved deep dimples in her plump cheeks.

Now, who did that remind him of? he thought sardonically.

He followed her gaze and felt a peculiar fizzing sensation, like pins and needles in his head, as he saw Sarah. Wrapped in a towel, her hair still wet from the shower, she was leaning against the banister on the landing above. As she caught Lottie's eye her face broke into an answering smile.

The camera caught it all. The joy and pride that shone from her face, the shimmer of tears in her eyes, her lips as they mouthed the words 'you're beautiful' at her little daughter and pressed a kiss to her fingertips, which she blew down to her.

'Could we have the little bridesmaid down at the front, please?' said the photographer briskly and, with a last glance up at her mother, Lottie was hustled into position for the shot by Fenella. Lorenzo kept his lens trained on Sarah, trying to resist the temptation to zoom in on her glorious cleavage as she leaned over the banister, looking down.

The light had left her, and suddenly she just looked unbearably sad. Stricken almost.

A sudden burst of laughter echoed round the walls as the photographer said something to make the bridal party relax their stiff poses. Lorenzo's focus didn't waver, and as the others collapsed with laughter he caught the single tear that fell from above, glinting as brightly as the diamonds in the bride's tiara for a second before shattering on the floor.

When he looked up again Sarah had gone.

* * *

Quietly, carefully, Sarah shut the door to her room and leaned against it for a moment, her palms pressed to her cheeks as she struggled to suppress the sudden swell of emotion that had caught her offguard.

She never cried.

Crying got you nowhere, unless you were Angelica and could do it cleanly and gracefully and use it to gain advantage in all kinds of situations. For Sarah, whose face instantly took on a blotched and swollen appearance that lasted for hours, it was undignified and definitely best avoided.

But back there, just for a second she'd been absolutely flattened by a wave of annihilating emotion. For Lottie, who was so sweet and good that sometimes she literally took Sarah's breath away; but also for the perfection of the morning and the sense of anticipation of the day ahead; the whole champagne and cake and silk and roses celebration of love and togetherness. Beneath the expensive designer trappings there was something primitive about it; something deeply profound and momentous, and all of a sudden Sarah had felt as if she was standing at the gates to paradise, looking in through the bars and knowing they were locked to her forever.

Anyway, self-pity was yet another indulgence she just didn't have time for right now, along with putting conditioner on her hair and shaving her legs. She'd showered and washed her hair in record time, even for her, so it would be stupid to waste valuable minutes bemoaning the fact that she was almost thirty and undoubtedly facing a future of spinsterish celibacy.

Hardly surprising, she thought bleakly, struggling into the most hideously unglamorous knickers on the planet. They were flesh-coloured and designed to 'smooth away all those lumps and bumps for a slender silhouette', but utterly kill any possibility of a passionate encounter. Mind you, she thought sadly, she seemed to do a pretty good job of that on her own if last night was anything to go by.

Averting her gaze from the mirror, she grabbed her dress and quickly shrugged it on. It was a lilac silk shift dress she'd bought in the sales a couple of years ago when Rupert had promised to take her to the polo at Windsor. Those were the days when she'd been on a constant diet, convinced that if she was thin enough and smart enough Rupert would be miraculously shaken out of his overwhelming apathy and realise he was deeply in love with her.

Predictably, neither the trip to the polo nor the dazzling epiphany about how desirable she was had ever happened.

She was standing in front of the mirror, smoothing the dress over her rigid new 'slender silhouette', when a knock at the door made her jump.

'Come in.'

The door opened and Lorenzo appeared. He was holding a glass of champagne.

'For you.'

'Oh…gosh, thanks,' Sarah stammered, taking it from him awkwardly. 'But you didn't have to—'

'I just came to tell you that you don't need to worry about the cake and the oysters.'

'Really?' Her blotched face brightened. 'But how?'

'I called Gennaro. He'll bring a cake up here while everyone is in church.'

'And the oysters?'

'He wouldn't spare his staff for just anyone, but you made quite an impression yesterday. Alfredo's wife, Paola, will come over too, as long as she can bring her little boy. It's hardly an army, but it should help.' He hesitated, then reached out and lightly brushed her swollen upper lip with his thumb. 'With the work at least. I'm not sure about everything else.'

'No.' She sat down suddenly on the stool in front of the dressing table. 'For that I'd need a make-up artist and a miracle. But in the absence of either I'm grateful for the champagne. Thank you for bringing it up.'

Walking to the door, he shrugged. '*Figurati.*' Walking to the door he smiled wryly. 'I'm just relieved that this time you're dressed.'

'Yes. But let's face it, it would hardly have mattered if I wasn't,' she said sadly. 'There's not really much of me that's left to the imagination now, is there?'

'Don't you believe it,' he said drily. 'Come down when you're ready. I'll give you a lift to the church.'

# CHAPTER NINE

IT WAS a beautiful wedding.

Everyone said so. They whispered it to each other in the church, with the honeyed sunlight pouring down through the high-up windows and scattering dancing rainbow points of light from the diamonds in Angelica's heirloom tiara across the worn stone floor. They said it afterwards, as they spilled out into the fierce heat and were introduced to people they hadn't yet met from the other family. And later, when generous quantities of the excellent champagne bought by Guy had made everyone sentimental, they looked around the flower-decked *limonaia* and said it again.

Sarah came out of the kitchen carrying a tray laden with coffee in tiny gold-rimmed cups. The ordeal of lunch was over and had passed blessedly smoothly, thanks to Gennaro's menu advice, his cake and also his hulking, taciturn kitchen assistant. Sarah had been so busy overseeing everything that she hadn't actually had time to sit down and eat, but from the empty plates Alfredo's pretty wife, Paola, was bringing back into the kitchen she could tell that the food had been a success.

Now the hard, enamel-blue sky had lost some of its glare and was beginning to soften to the shade of forget-me-nots, but it was still horribly hot. The *limonaia* looked like Titania's bower, and the scent of orange blossom and lilies and jasmine was enough to knock you out. Some people had moved outside, abandoning empty glasses and coffee cups for Sarah to find all around the courtyard and the top part of the garden, while others moved away from the places they'd been allocated at lunch and regrouped around the tables.

'Thank you, you're a saint,' sighed one of Hugh's aunts as Sarah put a coffee cup down in front of her. *St Knickerless,* thought Sarah wearily. It was so hot in the kitchen that she'd admitted defeat and put comfort before vanity, nipping upstairs an hour ago and taking off the punishing magic knickers.

'Beautiful wedding,' said the aunt.

'Yes.' Dutifully Sarah rested the tray on the edge of the table and surreptitiously leant her knee on the chair, taking the weight off one aching foot for a moment. 'It was so terrible to have to rearrange everything at the last minute, but—'

'Typical of Hugh and Angelica to turn a disaster round and make it into something positive,' said the aunt warmly, taking a sip of her coffee. 'They're so clever at that sort of thing. Angelica has a knack of doing everything brilliantly, and making it look so effortless, doesn't she?'

'Well, y-yes…I suppose so.' Sarah looked across at Angelica, who was holding court to three of Hugh's best-looking friends at the top table. 'Effortless is certainly the word.'

'And how do you know her?' said the aunt politely.

'I'm her sister.'

With an inward sigh Sarah waited for the inevitable, unflattering surprise. It came as expected.

'*Really?* Good lord, you don't look a bit alike. Her *sister?*'

'Well, half-sister,' Sarah explained dully. 'Different fathers.'

That was an understatement. Francis Tate and Guy Halliday were so different they were basically unrecognisable as the same species. No one could accuse Martha of falling for the same type.

At that moment a flash of white through the open doors of the *limonaia* caught her eye. Lottie, running across the lawn beyond the courtyard, her silk dress billowing out around her.

Another small figure darted after her—a little dark-haired boy. Sarah seized her chance of escape and straightened up.

'If you'll excuse me, I'll just go and see if my daughter—'

But, unwilling to be left stranded at the table with no one to talk to, the aunt wasn't ready to relinquish her yet. 'Ah, she's yours, is she, the little bridesmaid?' she said warmly. 'Isn't she adorable? Is your husband here?'

Sarah had seen that coming, like a ten-ton lorry lumbering towards her that she was powerless to avoid. She opened her mouth to reply—

'There you are, *tesoro*. I was looking for you.'

A warm hand came to rest on her shoulder, the thumb caressing her neck.

'Oh!' It was little more than a breathless gasp. She turned her head, vaguely noticing the expression on Hugh's aunt's face, which was one of respectful incredulity. But as she turned to face Lorenzo she forgot everything in the intensity of his dark eyes as they locked with hers, the very slight smile that touched the corners of his mouth.

She felt weak.

'Will you excuse us, *signora?*' Lorenzo murmured.

How, Sarah thought breathlessly, did he manage to sound so polite and at the same time so bloody sexy? His hand was firm on her elbow as he steered her towards the door. She arranged her face into what she hoped was an extremely nonchalant smile and said, without moving her lips, 'Why did you do that? She'll think you're my husband now.'

Lorenzo's voice was low, husky. 'I heard what she said. I thought that you needed rescuing.'

It was cooler outside. Sarah's heart was thudding hard and she was conscious of his closeness, of the height and strength of his body beside hers, the warmth of his hand on her bare arm. Too conscious. Although it went against just about every instinct in her tired being, she stopped walking and gently pulled her arm away.

'Look,' she said awkwardly, her voice low, 'you don't have to do that all the time, you know.'

They were standing in the shade of the kitchen wall. From inside she could hear water splashing in the sink and crashing pans, and from the other direction, from the *limonaia,* the sound of voices and laughter and glasses clinking. But here, in the middle, with the gardens rolling away in front of them, it was very quiet.

'Do what?'

'Rescue me.' She looked out across the lawn, watching Lottie and her mysterious new friend play beneath the trailing fronds of a weeping willow in the distance. 'I can look after myself.'

He gave a harsh, abrupt laugh. 'I don't think so.'

She froze. For a second it was all she could do to keep upright as anger and hurt exploded inside her, momentarily filling her head with blinding white light. Stepping backwards, staggering slightly, she put her hand against the wall for support.

'Well, I can. I always have, and tomorrow when this is all over I'll leave here and get on with doing just that again.'

Pushing past him, she headed back to the familiar safety of the kitchen.

Lorenzo slammed his fist against the wall, cursing viciously and eliciting a look of great alarm from a passing wedding guest.

What was it about Sarah Halliday that made him screw up *so* spectacularly every time he spoke to her?

*Dio,* he was used to dealing with demanding producers, bolshy film crews and Hollywood A-list actresses, who were surely some of the most volatile, egocentric, emotionally unstable people on the planet, and he was renowned in the business for his ability to get them to do what he wanted. But put him in front of this girl—this ordinary, unassuming, self-deprecating girl— and suddenly his responses were all over the place.

He hadn't meant it to sound like that. He hadn't meant to

put her down—she had her family for that, *per l'amore de Dio,* and he'd seen how she not only looked after her child, but the whole useless, lazy lot of them too. He'd simply meant that she put herself last. Always.

And that he didn't like it.

He shook his head, suddenly noticing the throbbing in his knuckles where they'd hit the stone. God, what a fool, he thought bleakly as he gingerly flexed his aching fingers. What a bloody stupid thing to have done.

Although actually, when you looked at it in context of the greater scheme of things, punching a wall wasn't so bad. After all, he actually had the girl who owned the rights to the film he'd been wanting to make for the last fifteen years right there in his house. Right there in his arms, at one memorable point. And he hadn't even got around to mentioning it yet.

That was even more stupid.

He inhaled, deeply and rapidly, and leaned back against the wall. Most stupid of all was the fact that with everything he said to her, everything he did, he seemed to be making it more and more difficult to bring the subject up, and more and more likely that if he did she would tell him exactly what he could do with his film. And now time was running out. Tomorrow, as she said, she would be leaving.

Shouts of children's laughter drifted through the drowsy afternoon. It was a sound not previously heard in the elegant formality of Castellaccio's gardens. Not by him, anyway, although the *palazzo* itself had been here for five hundred years, so countless children must have run across its lawns and shrieked with excitement as they played hide-and-seek in the trees. Through a dappling of leaves at the end of the lawn he could see the pale glimmer of Lottie's dress as she ran, chased by Alfredo's little boy, and before he had time to think about what he was doing he found himself walking across the lawn towards them, a plan half forming in his mind.

Not so much a plan as an impulse, actually. Like a plan, but less sensible. Less logical. And with a lot more potential for disaster.

'Mummy, this is Dino. He's my new friend.'

Sarah put down the dripping roasting pan she was about to dry and pushed one limp curl back from her forehead as she turned to face Lottie. Lottie, and a dark-haired little boy with eyes like molten chocolate. She gave him a tired smile.

'Hello, Dino. It's very nice to meet you.'

Dino smiled back, but shot a sideways glance at Lottie, who explained, 'Dino doesn't speak English, but he's teaching me Italian. I already know the words for hello and moon. Moon is *luna*.'

Sarah rolled her eyes and grinned. 'Trust you to find that one out first.'

'New moon is *luna nuova*. Did you know there's one tonight? We've told Auntie Angelica to make a wish on it, and I've wished for a telescope and a new teacher next year who's nicer than mean old Mrs Pritchard.' Lottie took hold of Sarah's soapy hand and tugged it. 'It's your turn now. Will you come and wish on it?'

'Wait!' Sarah protested. 'I've got all these horrible pans to wash. Couldn't you two do it for me? I'd like you to wish for...' she hesitated, ruthlessly suppressing the little voice inside her head that was whispering wicked things about Lorenzo Cavalleri. She laughed uneasily '...gosh, I don't know...world peace, and a big tub of chocolate fudge-brownie ice cream?'

'It won't work if we do it,' Lottie said stubbornly. There was a glint in her eye that Sarah recognised with a sinking heart as meaning she was Up To Something. 'You have to come and do it yourself. Maybe you could wish for the pans to wash themselves, and when you get back they'll all be done. Come on, Mummy.'

Lottie gave another pull on her hand, and as she followed reluctantly after her and Dino Sarah was torn between amusement and irritation. There was no stopping Lottie once she got an idea into her head, but tonight Sarah really wasn't in the mood. She was tired and hot and...hungry, she realised with a jolt of surprise. She couldn't remember the last time she'd eaten.

But more than all of that she was sad. Lorenzo had been so good to all of them, and she had thanked him by losing her temper like some spoiled schoolgirl, taking out on him her anger at herself. And tomorrow she would be leaving, and would never see him again.

The thought drove icicles into her heart.

She was surprised to find that it was almost dark outside. She must have been in the kitchen for longer than she'd thought, during which time the jazz quartet that Hugh had booked had arrived. As Lottie led her across the courtyard 'The Way You Look Tonight' was drifting out of the *limonaia,* where the candles had been lit on the tables. The purple evening was filled with the lovely, languid music, the muted sound of conversation and the scent of orange blossom.

Little Dino raced ahead of them, his white shirt the only part of him that was visible in the velvety gloom. Sarah stumbled after them, Lottie's hand warm and soft in hers.

*'Li e! La luna! Esprimi un desiderio!'*

Dino's voice broke into her thoughts and she looked up to where he was pointing. The delicate curve of a new moon was hanging in the sky, at the melting point where it changed from dark indigo to paler violet. A single star was placed with tasteful understatement, just to the right of it.

'You have to close your eyes,' said Lottie firmly, 'and I'm going to turn you round three times and then you have to make your wish, OK?'

The children's laughter bubbled up around her as the world darkened and spun. The ground seemed to rise and fall beneath her feet as she pirouetted.

'Now, wish!' Lottie trilled. 'Open your eyes and wish!'

Sarah opened her eyes, but instead of seeing the silvery new moon in the sky she found that she was facing the other way. Ahead of her, across the grass and encircled by the dark shapes of trees, stood the temple Lottie had told her about yesterday. The rest of the garden was shrouded in shadows, layers of inky blue and grey and mauve, but golden light spilled from between the four columns that supported its ornate portico.

Confused, she turned her head. The moon was behind her, its single star seeming to wink at her conspiratorially. And then she looked back, towards the temple, and saw a dark shape detach itself from one of the pillars and step forward into the flickering light.

Lorenzo.

# CHAPTER TEN

HER heart lurched and blood thundered in her ears, so that for a moment the music floating across the lawn was drowned out by a swishing, pounding beat. Lottie slipped her hand into Sarah's, and whispered, 'Did you wish, Mummy?'

'I—I don't know. Perhaps.'

Lottie was pulling her forward again, towards the temple, Dino following at their heels. 'We made a surprise for you.'

He straightened up as they approached. Sarah felt her pulse quicken and her mouth go dry as she stared through the gloom, taking in the long legs and broad shoulders silhouetted against the golden light.

'Lottie, what's all this about? I hope you haven't been bothering Lorenzo with—'

'They haven't. It was my idea.'

He was standing at the top of the flight of wide stone steps that led up to the columned portico. His face was unsmiling, reserved, but she thought she heard a subdued note of contrition in his voice.

'What was?'

He came down the steps towards her, his hand outstretched. Sarah's stomach disappeared and her breath caught in her throat as it closed around hers.

'Dinner.'

Gently he drew her forward. The stone steps were cool

under her feet, and as she reached the top she gave a gasp of astonishment.

There was a stone bench seat running along the back wall of the small square building, and at each end of it stood an elaborate candelabra holding out armfuls of flickering white candles. In the middle was a champagne bottle in an ice bucket and, on the floor beside it, an old-fashioned picnic hamper.

Her eyes flew to his face. He was watching her with his dark, hooded, unfathomable eyes. Her hand was still held in his, and it felt as if a low-level current of electricity was buzzing through their loosely entwined fingers. She pulled away, wrapping her arms around her body.

'I don't know what to say,' she whispered.

'Say you love it!' Lottie squealed, clapping her hands. 'It's like a fairy grotto!' She and Dino had crept up the steps after them and were standing side by side, looking at them both with dark eyes that shone with reflected light.

'I love it,' Sarah whispered. 'I do. But I don't know why you—'

He cut her off, turning to the children and taking something out of his pocket to give to them. '*Grazie mille, bambini.* Now, both of you, remember what we agreed? Lottie, you go straight to your grandmother. *Dino, trova il tuo madre, si?*'

'*Si!*' they chorused, clutching the coins that he had given them and turning to hurry down the steps. The sound of their voices carried across the darkening garden as they ran back towards the house, Lottie's dress melting, moth-like, into the gloom.

Sarah watched them until they were out of sight. And then slowly, inexorably she felt her gaze being pulled back to Lorenzo. He was still looking at her, and there was something almost sad in his expression that turned Sarah's heart over.

'I don't understand,' she said slowly.

'I wanted to apologise. I didn't mean what I said before.' He sighed. 'Or I did mean it, but not in the way it sounded. Not in the way you thought. I don't think for one minute you're incapable of looking after yourself, just that you don't put your own needs first.'

She shook her head dismissively. 'It doesn't matter. I'm fine.'

'Have you eaten today?'

'N-no, but—'

'*Essattamente.*' He stooped to open the lid of the basket. 'You look after everyone else. You feed them.' Sitting down, he took out a box and put it beside him on the stone seat. 'You clear up after them. You organise things for them. You even risk your neck doing property maintenance for them. But what I want to know is…' he opened the box and took out an oyster and a short, heavy-handled knife '…who looks after you?'

His voice was very quiet, very gentle. Mesmerised, she watched the movements of his strong, slender hands.

'I told you. I don't need looking after. Really, I don't. I've always been independent. I'd hate to have someone bossing me around and telling me what to do.'

'Sit down.'

She came over and, without thinking, sat. His lips quirked into a fleeting smile, and she laughed.

'OK, most of the time I'd hate it. Tonight I'm too tired to argue.'

Lorenzo slid the champagne bottle out of the bucket of iced water and tore the foil from the top. Sarah watched the icy drops of water run down over his fingers as he poured the clear, golden liquid into two glasses.

'That's a relief,' he said drily, handing one to her, 'but hardly a surprise. You've run today entirely single-handedly, from what I've seen. It can't be easy taking responsibility for everything on your own.'

'I'm used to it. As I said, Lottie's father was never around much.'

'I know. But I get the impression you've been shouldering responsibility for a lot longer than that,' he said quietly.

The darkness that was gathering outside seemed to swoop

in on her suddenly, crowding into her heart, dragging it down with that familiar, crushing weight. The terrible weight of responsibility.

How had he seen that?

She took a large gulp of champagne. She didn't want to look at him. She was frightened of what else he might see.

He was holding an oyster, cupping it in his big, sensitive hands as he slipped the knife in and turned it swiftly, prising the two halves of the shell apart. Sarah watched as the oyster split open. He held it out to her.

She hesitated. 'I'm not sure… It sounds ridiculous, but I've never tried one before.'

'Your life has been far too sheltered, Miss Halliday,' he said solemnly. 'First Screaming Orgasms and now oysters. There are huge gaps in your education.'

They were sitting side by side on the long stone bench, but Sarah found that she had subconsciously turned towards him, her knee hitched up on the seat. He hardly had to reach at all to offer the oyster to her lips. Instinctively, tentatively she felt them part. Her eyes met his and locked there and she felt herself melting into their velvet depths.

'You take it into your mouth,' he said softly, 'and hold it there. Don't chew. Crush it on your tongue.'

Her eyes never left his as she did as he said. Taste exploded in her mouth as it was filled with the cool, slippery, salty flesh and an answering explosion of lust rocked through her pelvis, partly at the undeniably erotic flavour of the oyster, partly at the flare of warmth she saw in the depths of his eyes. All of a sudden the heat of the evening seemed to be concentrated in the apex of her thighs.

'Now swallow,' he said huskily.

*Oh, God. Oh, help.*

'You liked that?'

'Yes,' she breathed. 'Oh, yes…'

He picked up another one, turning it over in his hand before plunging the knife in. 'So, Sarah Halliday, what is it that gave you such a big sense of responsibility?'

Taking a long, dizzying mouthful of champagne, she was caught off guard by his unexpected question. As the bubbles prickled and died on her tongue, she put her glass down, twisting its slender stem between her fingers.

'I don't know. My father...'

She stopped abruptly, a little thud of shock spreading through her as those two words brought her back to her senses. She was tired, both physically and mentally, after the stresses of Angelica's wedding day, and there was something about the combination of the champagne, the candles, the heat of the evening and of his steady, intense gaze that was making her feel raw. If she wasn't careful she'd be spilling out the whole unedifying story of her life and boring him senseless.

Beside her, Lorenzo tipped the oyster into his mouth and let its feral, female flavour seep onto his tongue while he waited for her to continue. *Dio,* he'd known this would be difficult, but he'd failed to take into account the oysters. Eating them while looking into her dark, dilated eyes was like torment.

But this was it. He'd got her to the place he needed to be.

'What about your father?' he said, with what he hoped was almost indifference. 'Tell me about him.'

She shook her head with a swift vehemence that was both intriguing and frustrating. 'It's a long story. A long, not very interesting story.'

'Can I be the judge of that?'

Trying not to betray his interest, Lorenzo selected an oyster from the pile and looked at it, assessing where to put the tip of the knife in. People said oysters were difficult to open, but in his experience it was just a matter of knowing where to start. He found a gap and gently eased the blade in.

'Take my word for it.' Sarah spoke lightly, but her words were edged with weariness and despair. 'Other people's family dramas are always tedious. They're all just variations on the same old themes, aren't they?'

'And what themes are those?' He gave the knife a little twist and felt a beat of satisfaction as the shell gave. He was in.

'Guilt, regret, loss…'

Her words trailed off as he held the oyster up to her mouth. Her pink lips parted, and he watched her face, an arrow of lust skewering him at the expression of focused, private pleasure that flickered across it for a moment as she held the flesh in her mouth, and then let it slide down her throat.

'You loved him?' His voice was a hoarse rasp.

Outside the evening had deepened softly into night. The hopeful sliver of the new moon was too high for them to see it from beneath the canopy of the temple, too small to shed any light over the sleeping garden. It was as if the rest of the world had vanished, and it was just the two of them.

Sarah's eyes met his, and behind the shimmering candlelight reflected in them lay a continent of hurt.

'Yes, I loved him,' she said quietly.

Lorenzo swept the oyster shells back into the box and poured more champagne. The bottle rattled slightly against the rim of Sarah's glass, and he realised that his hands were shaking. He had to get a grip. Stay focused. This was his chance

'So where do guilt and regret fit in?' he said neutrally, picking up his glass and leaning back. *Don't pressure her. Don't make her feel threatened.*

'I obviously didn't show him enough. I should have done more.'

Lorenzo made himself take a long sip of champagne. 'How old were you when he died?'

She was sitting very still, her head bent. One heavy chestnut curl fell in front of her face. The candlelight made it shine like polished copper. 'I was five.'

'Like Lottie.' Lorenzo's heart clenched unexpectedly.

'Yes,' she whispered.

Carefully he set his glass down and leaned forward, stroking the curl gently to the side, tucking it behind her ear. 'That's a big burden for a little girl to carry. What makes you think you should have done more?'

'He killed himself.'

'*Ah, piccolino.*' The words escaped Lorenzo's lips stealthily on an outward breath, and his fingers tingled with the sudden urge to take her face between his hands and kiss away the frown between her delicately traced brows, the shadows beneath her eyes. He held back. He had to keep her talking, to get to a point where he could bring up the subject of the book...

Her head remained bent, her arms tightly folded, almost as if she was making herself as small and as still as possible. 'If I had been more...' she went on very hesitantly, 'I don't know...*more*...then maybe he wouldn't have done it. He wrote this book, you see, and it was kind of his life's work. He dedicated it to me, and the dedication says something about how I made his whole life worthwhile...' She stopped and gave a bitter laugh. 'At some point shortly after that he must have changed his mind, or maybe I just stopped making his life worthwhile.'

Lorenzo felt as if he'd been turned to stone. *I know,* he should be saying, *I know about the book*, but suddenly, in the face of her misery and despair, and her dreadful, unjustified guilt, it simply didn't seem important. What mattered was her.

He shook his head, slowly, emphatically. 'You can't blame yourself,' he said softly. 'He was a grown man, with all kinds of reasons that we might never know or understand to be unhappy. When things get that bad it's impossible to think clearly, or to grasp the consequences of your actions. He wasn't in any position to understand what he was doing.'

She hesitated, then slowly raised her head and looked at him. 'I wish I could believe that.'

Her voice was oddly flat, but her eyes were pools of anguish and as he looked into them Lorenzo realised he was staring into the dark and secret heart of her. Somewhere here lay the key to who she was, and why, and he wanted very much to find it.

His heart was thudding against his ribs and he said, very gently, 'It's OK to be angry, Sarah.'

The instant flare of emotion there told him he was right. She moved, leaning back against the stone wall, tucking her legs up against her body and wrapping her arms around them as she looked out into the darkness beyond their circle of gold.

'It's not,' she said hollowly. 'I have so little of him. I had so little time with him and now I have so little to remember him by that it's not OK to spoil that by being angry. It's awful.'

'No, it's *natural*. Completely natural. That's what the guilt is about too, isn't it? Not because you blame yourself, but because you blame him?'

She nodded, and he saw her stiff shoulders sag a little. 'A bit. Afterwards, when my mother married Guy, I used to wish he was my real father. He was what a proper father should be. Always laughing and pulling wads of money out of his pockets and calling Angelica "princess". But I do blame myself too. I wasn't sunny and golden and gorgeous like Angelica. I was this painfully shy, awkward child.'

'You were *his* child. He would have loved you for what you were.'

She looked at him, frowning, and for a breathless, agonising moment he thought she'd heard the wistfulness he'd tried to hide behind the words. But then she smiled, a brief, twisted echo of her familiar swift smile.

'I wasn't enough,' she said with heavy irony.

Lorenzo sighed, leaning over and taking a plate with a generous wedge of wedding cake from the basket on the floor. 'Children can't be responsible for the happiness of their parents. You know that. Is it Lottie's fault that her father didn't stay around?'

'No. No, that's my fault too.' She made a brave attempt at a laugh. 'Oh, God, listen to me. I'm hardly the world's most scintillating dinner companion at the best of times, but I'm not usually this dull. Let's have some of Gennaro's cake and talk about something else.'

As she spoke, a single, shining tear ran down her cheek. Before he knew what he was doing Lorenzo had closed the gap between them and was cupping her warm face, rubbing away the glistening salt-trail with his thumb.

'We are going to have some cake,' he said softly, 'but we're not changing the subject until we've got a few things straight.' He could feel her trembling beneath his palm. 'One—it's not your fault that Lottie's father didn't stay. It's not even his fault. It's his *loss*.'

Her eyelids closed for a second, an expression of pain flickering over her face. He waited for her to argue, but the seconds ticked by and she said nothing, and he felt an almost visceral pull of satisfaction.

Maybe he was starting to reach her. Maybe she was listening.

He took a spoonful of cake and held it up to her lips. Her head was tipped back against the wall, her luxuriant hair fanning out like a mantle behind her, and she watched him with dark, unreadable eyes as she opened her mouth.

His whole body was thrumming with adrenaline and desire and the effort of not kissing her. 'And two,' he went on, his voice little more than a husky whisper now, 'you're not dull. You're one of the most complicated, interesting people I've met in a long time.'

He shifted his position slightly, wedging his shoulder against the wall right beside her and turning his body towards hers. He sank the spoon into the creamy cake and gave her another mouthful, which she took as pliantly as a child. Her eyes were on his, smudged and shadowed with exhaustion. Tentatively trusting.

In the distance he could hear music, reaching them faintly from the wedding. Darkness lay in veils of purple and blue over the garden and a tentative enchantment lay over their golden temple, where the candles cast flickering shadows on the worn stone and enfolded them both. Beside him he could hear the soft sigh of Sarah's breathing, and was aware of the slow rise and fall of her chest.

Ruthlessly, gritting his teeth, he turned his thoughts away from her chest.

'*Sarah…*' he said softly, thoughtfully, as if he were turning the word over in his hands and examining it. 'Pretty name.'

She gave a tiny, sad smile. 'Not as pretty as Angelica.'

'Very different. Was it your father's choice?'

A tiny shake of her head made her rich hair glitter with a thousand golden lights. 'My mother's,' she said sleepily. 'And Angelica was too. She loves ang—' She stopped, sighed, slowly looked up at him, with huge troubled eyes. 'Angels,' she whispered. 'She loves angels.'

Lorenzo had the strangest sensation of his heart being squeezed as realisation dawned. 'Seraphina,' he said very softly.

Her eyes closed. She gave the barest nod, the shadows emphasising the dimple in her cheek as that fleeting smile touched her lips. 'It doesn't suit me. I can't live up to it. I'm much more of a Sarah.'

He put the spoon down, and moved a little so that her head was on his shoulder. She gave a tremulous, shuddering sigh, but didn't resist, and lay very still against him as he stroked her hair.

Minutes passed, stretching into longer, measureless spaces of time. The candles dipped and guttered in the little breeze, the music stopped and the darkness was opaque and silent. There was just her breathing, her soft hair, her generous, pliant body that smelled of soap and sweetness. Still he kept stroking, slow and rhythmical. It didn't matter that she was asleep. He wanted to do it anyway. For her.

# CHAPTER ELEVEN

LORENZO sat at his desk, idly toying with the orrery.

It was a mechanical model of the solar system, showing everything in its relative position. There was something soothing about watching how the moons and planets followed their own unwavering path, each one taking its own specific place in a dance so intricate it was almost beyond human comprehension. Galileo had understood it, even though it went against everything he'd been brought up to believe.

The courage of that, the audacious brilliance never failed to impress Lorenzo. Galileo had had a vision, and he had been unswerving in his pursuit of it. But even he, with his towering intellect, had never fully got to grips with the complexities of women.

With a flick of his finger Lorenzo made the earth spin on its axis, and then slowed it right down again as he thought back to last night. That was how it had felt in the temple, in the candlelight and the silence. As if he had slowed down time. Stopped the world, for a little while.

From outside the study door the sound of the grandfather clock chiming the half-hour was a stark reminder of the foolishness of that illusion. His battered copy of *The Oak and the Cypress* lay on the desk in front of him and he picked it up now, frowning as he leafed through the first few pages to find the dedication.

*To Seraphina,*
*who gives me hope, joy and a reason for being.*

Lorenzo threw the book back down onto the desk and stood up with a sigh. Looking at those words now, he could understand how they could make her feel that she had failed somehow. That she was unworthy of unconditional love. That she had to earn everything.

Moving towards the window, he saw Lottie sitting on the grass that edged the gravel drive with Dino beside her. Lupo was lying a little way off, watching them as they half-heartedly threw bits of gravel at an empty juice carton they'd put beneath the study window. There was a downwards, dejected stoop to both small sets of shoulders, and as he looked more closely Lorenzo could see that Lottie had been crying. Her face was blotched with tears, and streaked with grime where she'd brushed them away with grubby hands.

As he watched she picked up another stone and threw it at the carton, but angrily this time; harder, so that it bounced up and hit the glass. She clapped a hand to her mouth, her eyes wide with horror, while beside her Dino scrambled to his feet and then pulled her up after him. A moment later they'd both scampered off.

Lorenzo turned away with a small smile. Switching on the music to break the oppressive silence, he returned to his desk, and the sunlit room filled with the swooping sound of strings and flute.

Antonio Agostino was a composer of Oscar-winning film scores. He had also been one of the first people Lorenzo had told about his plan to film Tate's book. After lending him a copy, this was one of the pieces Antonio had come up with for the film, and Lorenzo only had to close his eyes and he was back in Oxfordshire on that hot July evening, watching Sarah stride across the field of wheat as the last rays of the sun turned it to molten gold...

There was a knock on the door, and he opened his eyes with a start.

'*Entrare,*' he barked, much more harshly than he intended. For a moment nothing happened, and then very slowly, very hesitantly the door opened. After a couple more seconds Lottie and Dino shuffled in, their hands tightly clasped, their eyes downcast. Lupo skulked at their heels, his tale rammed between his legs.

'Sorry for throwing the stone,' said Lottie quietly. '*Mi dispace.*' Her chin wobbled as if she was holding back the tears by massive force of will. Lorenzo knew exactly where she got that strength from.

'*Non importa.* Nothing is broken,' he said roughly, suddenly finding that his throat felt tight. 'Your Italian is coming along very well. Has Dino been teaching you?'

She nodded, but at the same time her face crumpled and the tears welling in her eyes dripped down her cheeks.

Lorenzo frowned, feeling utterly helpless in the face of the little girl's misery. He knew nothing about children—had neither needed to nor wanted to before.

Self-defence. How stupid and cowardly that seemed now.

'What's the matter?' he said softly as he watched Dino put his arm protectively round her shaking shoulders. Perhaps he should take lessons from him, Lorenzo thought wearily. Dino's natural, empathetic manner seemed to be going down a lot better than his recent attempts at offering comfort to females in distress.

'I don't want to go,' Lottie sobbed. 'I hate London, and I hate the mean girls in my class. All they ever do is play with dolls with horrid, make-uppy faces and say nasty things about each other. I asked Mummy when we could come back here and she said we might not, and Dino is my *best friend* but I don't know if I'll see him again ever because we live thousands and thousands of miles away…'

'Shh…' Lorenzo said, painfully aware of how inadequate that was, but temporarily unable to think of anything more useful. Then he looked at the orrery.

'Come and look at this,' he said gravely, moving back

slightly so that they both had a clear view of the complex arrangement of spheres and dials. Lottie looked wary, but she sniffed and came closer.

'What is it? Is that the moon?'

'That big golden orb in the middle is the sun,' Lorenzo explained. 'The smaller one here is the moon and next to it, with the funny shapes all over it, is the earth.'

'Ohhh…'

Lottie let out a breath of awe. Tears still shimmered in her eyes, but her face now wore an expression of total absorption. At her shoulder Dino's smooth, olive face was serious too.

Lorenzo turned the tiny globe around. 'Look—here's Italia, and we're there, on this side, in Tuscany. And there…' he moved his finger upwards and to the left a fraction '…there is London. See? It isn't as far as you think. Not compared to all of this…' With a swift movement he set the globe spinning and leaned back, studying the look of wonder on the children's faces as they took in the blur of sea and land, spinning on its axis as the planets and their moons kept their silent course around it.

'Lottie?'

Lorenzo looked up. Sarah stood in the doorway. Her hair was tied back, and she was wearing a faded green T-shirt and a little denim skirt that showed off her long brown legs.

Lottie didn't turn around. 'What?' she said, with as much sullenness as she dared.

'You have to come and wash your face and hands now,' Sarah said gently.

Lottie stayed where she was and cast one more covetous glance at the orrery. 'Thank you for showing it to me,' she said, looking solemnly at Lorenzo before turning and walking very stiffly past her mother. Dino followed like a shadow at her heels, and even Lupo looked uncertain whether to stay or go.

Sarah hesitated in the doorway. 'Lorenzo, about last night…' she said with painful awkwardness. 'I'm so sorry. For boring you senseless and falling asleep on you. I don't know what came over me.'

'Extreme tiredness, I assume,' he said drily. 'You'd been working flat out all day. There's absolutely no need to apologise.'

Her head was bent and she was rubbing the brass doorknob with the tip of her finger. Her hair fell partly over her face, but he could still see that she was blushing fiercely. 'But you must have carried me to bed when I was asleep and…'

'*Si.*' He kept his voice deliberately nonchalant. 'It was a huge relief to be able to do something for you without you arguing.'

'Thank you,' she murmured in an agony of discomfort. Then, clearly at a loss for what to say next, she added, 'I hope the children haven't disturbed you too much.'

'No.' Why hadn't he noticed before what great legs she had? All of a sudden it seemed impossible to notice anything else.

'That's good.'

Sarah sighed. In the polished brass doorknob she could see the reflection of her face, looking very small and far away. 'Lottie's pretty angry with me at the moment.'

'Because you told her that she wouldn't be coming back to see Dino.'

Stung by the faintly accusing note in his voice, she let go of the door and straightened up. 'Yes, well, I don't believe in getting children's hopes up. And to be quite honest, I think it's unlikely. Angelica's love affair with the farmhouse seems to have come to an abrupt end. It's going to take so much work to put the roof right, so who knows if they'll keep it? And even if they do, air fares are expensive, especially in school holidays. Guy paid for us to come out here for the wedding, but a day trip to Brighton beach is about all we usually manage, so, all in all, I can't make any promises.'

Lorenzo looked thoughtful. 'She doesn't like school much, does she?'

The observation caught her off guard. There had been a part of her that wanted him to argue with her, to tell her that it wouldn't be so out of the question for her to return. Maybe even to make her feel as if he wanted her to.

'How do you know?'

He shrugged. 'Just something she said. She doesn't want to go back.'

'She doesn't have a choice, I'm afraid,' Sarah said bleakly. 'It's difficult for her, I know that, but I'd rather she was upset now and dealt with it instead of wasting time wishing and hoping for something that's not going to happen. It's best to be realistic.'

She wondered if he understood that she was talking about herself as much as Lottie.

Sitting at his desk, he listened with his head slightly bent, his gaze fixed straight in front of him. He waited until after she'd finished, and then after a little pause said, 'I want to offer you a choice.'

Time seemed to falter, as if the unseen hand that turned the cogs and made the planets move had slowed for a moment. Sarah felt the air catch in her throat, disrupting the rhythm of her breathing, forcing her to do an odd little gasp before she said, 'What do you mean?'

'I mean,' he said slowly, getting up and turning to face her properly, 'I want to ask you to stay. You need a job and I need—'

'*No*,' she said, instantly on the defensive. 'No, you can't do that.'

His eyebrows rose. 'Do what?'

'Rescue me again. I know that you're trying to help, but—'

'You seem to think I'm far more honourable than I really am,' he said, a faintly ironic smile touching his mouth. 'In this situation I'm the one who needs help. You know that I can't run this place on my own; that much has been obvious since the moment you arrived. I need someone to look after the house; you could do with the money, you love Italy and Lottie seems to like it here. What I'm suggesting is purely a business arrangement, for as long as you want—until the end of the summer when Lottie needs to go back to school, or longer.'

His tone was eminently, hypnotically reasonable, and after he finished speaking the room was very quiet. Dust motes swirled languidly in the streams of pale sunlight pouring through the elegant windows. Sarah watched them, trying to keep track of the same tiny individual speck as it drifted and spiralled on invisible currents of air.

It was impossible, of course. Just as it was impossible to take in what Lorenzo was saying. Up until a moment ago she had been preparing to leave, torn between wanting to imprint every detail of his face on her mind, memorise every movement and mannerism, and wanting to shut him out, walk away without looking back and try to forget.

And now this. This other *choice*.

'There's a project that I'm trying to get off the ground,' he began again, and a faint note of rare uncertainty in his voice snapped her attention right back to where he was standing by the desk, turning over a tattered and plainly bound book in his hands. 'It's at a delicate stage, but I want to make it happen. Very much.' He looked up at her and seemed to hesitate for a moment. Then he put the book down and went on more certainly, 'I'm going to be having meetings with producers and accountants and studios and backers, so I want to have someone around who can make a decent cup of coffee.'

'I don't know what to say.' Even to Sarah's own ears her voice sounded strange and distant. 'It's a bit unexpected.'

He nodded. 'Of course. Think about it. Talk to Lottie.'

'You think I'd get a balanced argument from her?' Sarah laughed shakily. 'She'd bite your hand off.'

'Then what's stopping you?'

He was looking at her. She could hear her own heartbeat; feel it, all over her body.

He turned away, gathering up a drift of papers from the desk and frowning slightly as he rustled them into a neat pile. 'You'll be completely free to do as you like. I'm going to be totally taken up with working on a script, so we probably won't even see that much of each other.'

His meaning was loud and clear. He was telling her that this was work. That there would be no more kissing in the kitchen or whispered confessions by candlelight. This was, as he said, a business arrangement. It was time to get back to reality.

Reality was London, and Rupert and Julia. It was the depressing flat with the nasty orange carpet she couldn't afford to replace and the tiny little yard that never got any sun. Reality was having to look for a job and explain about why she left the last one, and then worrying about who would look after Lottie in the holidays when she was working and how she was going to pay them.

Reality was a place where she had a lot of problems to deal with, and just the thought of it made her feel exhausted and depressed. Lorenzo had just offered her the solution to all of those problems in a single stroke. The only thing that was standing in the way was her own pride and, since she could barely even afford to buy her daughter a pair of shoes, pride was looking like a luxury that was well out of her league.

She took a step away from the door, digging her nails into her palms as she forced herself to raise her head and look at him squarely. But she couldn't manage a smile.

'Thank you,' she said solemnly, sounding slightly breathless with the effort of keeping all the doubts and misgivings and other messy, inconvenient, unbusinesslike emotions in check. 'Yes, please. If you're sure you don't mind? I'd like to stay.'

# CHAPTER TWELVE

AT FIRST Sarah had felt awkward and uneasy being at Castellaccio after the rest of her family had left. Through the long, hot days the house was very still and quiet, almost seeming to hold its breath as she passed through the elegant rooms, as if it was wondering who she was, what she was doing there.

Sarah wondered that herself sometimes, but, while it took her a bit of time to adjust, Lottie took to her new surroundings like the proverbial duck. In the days following the departure of the whole Halliday family circus Sarah wistfully watched the solemn, solitary little girl she had known in London blossom into a wild little wood-nymph with sparkling eyes and cheeks as smooth and brown as conkers.

The crowning joy in Lottie's happiness was the bedroom Lorenzo had shown her to, just after Guy and Martha had left. Picking up the bag of her things that Sarah had packed in preparation for their own departure, Lorenzo had carried it upstairs and along the corridor to a small room right at the end; a small white cell with a long uncurtained window and a domed, blue-painted ceiling picked out with tiny, faded stars and a silver crescent moon.

Lottie and Dino spent every day together, mostly in the gardens of the *palazzo,* under the watchful eye of Alfredo, as he mowed and snipped and tidied. From the kitchen Sarah could hear the children's shrieks of laughter drifting across the lawn as they chased each other through the jet of the hosepipe. Sometimes she took them both down into the village to get supplies for dinner and bought them ice cream, which they ate in rare, reverent silence as they sat in the square, or sometimes she would leave them with Dino's gentle, patient mother, Paola, whom Lottie quickly came to adore.

By contrast Sarah felt as if she was existing in a state of suspended animation. Where Lottie had come vibrantly alive, Sarah drifted, ghostlike, through each day, barely thinking beyond the moment, and certainly no further than the next meal. It was, she recognised, a self-defence mechanism, and part of the magic of Castellaccio. The peace of the place, the beauty and tranquillity were so far removed from all the problems she had left behind in London that it was as if she were looking at them through the wrong end of a telescope.

Ironically, this diminished scale on her old life gave her a much clearer perspective on it. As the days stretched into weeks she thought of Rupert less and less often, and when she did it was with increasing anger and contempt, and she wondered how she had ever thought she loved him. He had given her Lottie, and for that inadvertent blessing she was profoundly, dizzyingly grateful, but, looking back, she found it astonishing to realise how little else he had given her; how little she had asked or expected from him. Not materially; she didn't care that he had never bought her jewellery or presents, but now, in the evenings as she cooked for Lorenzo and as they sat together in the warm dusk, she understood for the first time how much she had missed having someone to talk to. Another adult with whom to discuss little details of the day, to share the latest funny development in the hybrid Anglo-Italian language Lottie and Dino seemed to be inventing, to appreciate her cooking.

By some tacit agreement their conversation was always general and impersonal. He didn't talk much about himself, and there was no repeat of the night in the temple when she had bared her soul to his tender, merciless scrutiny. But still, every day Sarah found herself looking forward to the evening, after Dino had gone home and Lottie was bathed and sweetly asleep beneath her dome of painted stars, when Lorenzo would emerge from his study and they would eat together and drink cool, sharp wine as the evening darkened around them.

Sometimes he didn't finish working until late and, heart hammering, she would knock on the door to his study to tell him that dinner was ready. Often he was on the phone when she went in, or so absorbed in whatever it was he was working on that he hadn't noticed the time, and then he would scowl and lean back in his chair, stretching his powerful, rangy body like a panther, and her heart would flip as she noticed the lines of exhaustion carved into his face, the shadows beneath his eyes. In those unguarded moments she would glimpse whirlpools of emotion in their dark depths. But then the shutters would come down and he would pour wine and talk and be himself—interesting, incisive, amusing, and she would ache helplessly for him and the loneliness he wouldn't share.

It was only natural that she should care about him, she told herself firmly as she lay awake on the hot nights when sleep eluded her. They were friends. He had done so much for both her and Lottie, more than she could ever thank him for. He had helped her to get over her broken heart—or at least helped her to realise that it wasn't really broken at all—so it was perfectly reasonable that she should want to help him in return. But staring into the velvety summer darkness, listening to the faint strains of music drifting out from his study, she would twist between the burning sheets, wracked with terrible longing that had nothing to do with friendship.

One evening as she came downstairs from putting Lottie to bed she heard the phone ringing in the kitchen. This wasn't uncommon, and usually she left it for Lorenzo to pick up in his study, but as she crossed the hallway she heard the low rumble of his voice through the study door and realised he must be on the other line. Breaking into a run, she reached it and picked up, only realising as she gasped 'hello' that if the voice on the other end was Italian she was going to be no use whatsoever as a message-answering service.

'Hello. Who's that?'

Clearly Italian, but speaking English. Thank goodness. 'Oh, um…it's Sarah. I'm Signor Cavalleri's…housekeeper.'

Relief added to Sarah's breathlessness, made her doubly incoherent. In sharp contrast to the husky, beautifully modulated voice on the other end of the line.

'*Bene.* I'm very glad to hear it, Sarah. Thank goodness he's seen sense and got someone in to look after the place. And him. Would it be possible to speak with him?'

Sarah found she was gripping the phone tightly and her palms were sticky as she recognised that sexy, slow voice with its American-accented English. It wasn't every day you had a conversation with a Hollywood legend after all. 'I'm afraid he's on the other line at the moment. Is that Signora Cavalleri? I can ask him to call you back when he's…'

She stopped. Lorenzo was standing in the doorway, his face an expressionless mask. 'Oh! Wait a moment…'

He scowled, shaking his head, but it was too late. The words had already left her mouth. 'He's just here. Hold on.

'Oh, God, I'm sorry,' she murmured as he came towards her and took the phone. His expression was still perfectly blank, but a muscle flickered in his cheek.

'*Ciao,*' he said tonelessly, turning his back on Sarah.

She stumbled outside into the hazy twilight. The days were still scorchingly hot and dry, but in the three weeks since she'd been here the evenings seemed to be falling earlier and bringing with them a breath of cool air that heralded the distant approach of autumn. August was nearly over, she thought with a shiver. Soon she would have to rouse herself from the comforting torpor that had got her through the last few weeks and make some decisions about the future.

She didn't want to go home, she admitted to herself with a

thud of painful resignation. She had felt more at peace here in the last three weeks than she had in the last three years in London. She was content, and Lottie was properly happy. There really wasn't a decision to be made.

She bent down, running a head of lavender through her fingers and inhaling its evocative scent as she tried not to listen to the rise and fall of Lorenzo's beautiful voice in the kitchen. Not that she could understand a word of what he was saying, but just standing in the warm dusk, closing her eyes and listening to the ribbons of husky Italian thread themselves around her was so deliciously sensual that it felt illicit.

It's because he's talking to Tia, she reminded herself crossly, opening her eyes again. No wonder he sounds sensual—he's still crazy about her, along with half the male population of the planet. There was one word she did recognise, actually, and he kept saying it. *Venezia.* Maybe they were talking about giving things another go and planning a romantic reunion in Venice?

Barbs of anguish snagged at her and she wrapped her arms around herself and strode quickly out across the grass, not slowing her pace until she got out of hearing range of the house. The grass was soft and springy beneath her feet, and she looked down at her toes, still with the same lettuce-green nail varnish on them, sinking into the mossy ground. Noticing the nail varnish suddenly transported her back to that day in the square when Lorenzo had taken her out to lunch and talked to her.

Really talked, as though he was interested in her and Lottie and her father…

What would happen if Tia de Luca came back now? she thought miserably. There was no way she'd want a couple of strays taken in by her husband around the place, so perhaps Sarah and Lottie would be heading back to London after all.

Of course, she would be glad for Lorenzo, she thought fiercely. If Tia came back maybe his eyes would finally lose that empty look, and he wouldn't need to work fourteen hours a day to blot out the loneliness. God, she more than anyone understood about loneliness. She wouldn't wish it on anyone, and Lorenzo deserved so much to be happy. Yes. She cared for him, as a friend, and she wanted him to be happy...

She stopped walking suddenly, giving a whimper of distress as she realised where she was. In front of her, the last rays of the sinking sun painting it a glowing shade of apricot-pink, stood the temple.

Slowly she went up the stone steps, and stood between the pillars. The floor was worn and uneven, and some of the flag-stones were cracked. She hadn't been down here since that night when Lorenzo had fed her and held her and she'd fallen asleep in his arms.

She hadn't allowed herself to think about it much either. It took her down shadowy, twisting, forbidden pathways that led a long way from the straight and narrow road marked 'business arrangement', but now she felt a gentle blush spread over her skin as she let herself remember. Remember the bliss of finally relaxing; of surrendering the burden and letting someone else carry it for her. Lorenzo was fathom-lessly wise and incredibly strong, and he had listened and understood. And afterwards he had fed her gently and stroked her hair.

But it was what she didn't remember that bothered her. The bit where he must have picked her up and carried her through the darkness to the house...

The blush intensified to a deep, searing glow that radiated heat through her whole body, and she wrapped her arms round a cool stone pillar. She had woken in her own bed the next morning. He must have taken her dress off, but she still wore her underwear...

Her bra, anyway. Of course, she'd taken the ugly knickers off earlier. She was miserably undecided about whether that was a good thing or not.

'There you are.'

Letting go of the pillar quickly, she looked round. Lorenzo

was walking across the lawn towards her, a bottle of wine held in one hand, two glasses loosely clasped in the other. As he approached she scanned his face. He looked distracted and tired, and not particularly like a man who had just arranged a romantic reunion with his ex-wife. But, of course, they had a lot of stuff to sort out. Maybe he wasn't allowing himself to get too hopeful.

'I need to talk to you,' he said, coming up the steps.

A chill went through her. 'Right.' Irrationally she found herself wishing she'd washed her hair and that she wasn't wearing the same coral-pink shirt again. The clothes she had packed for her four-day stay at the farmhouse were doing sterling service, but she was getting heartily sick of them. She had a sudden fleeting image of Tia de Luca in her silken tunic in the magazine—exotic, sophisticated, edgy.

Lorenzo set the glasses down on the stone bench in almost the same place as last time. Sarah found herself reluctant to sit down. Instead she stayed leaning up against the pillar, her arms folded protectively across her body.

His hair was longer now, and as he bent his head to pour the wine it fell forward and she could see the streaks of grey at his temples. She felt a wrenching sensation in her chest.

'Is Lottie asleep?' he asked, coming forward and handing her a glass of pale wine.

'Yes, finally.' She took the glass from him, talking quickly to cover up her awkwardness. 'She was full of all these elaborate plans that she and Dino have been hatching together for a sleepover, in a tent. Apparently Alfredo has said that he'll stay out with them and they'll have a midnight feast of ice cream and cook sausages for breakfast. It's all very exhausting.'

Lorenzo raised an eyebrow. 'But well thought-out. Have you agreed?'

'I said I'd ask you. Sorry—I forgot to mention that they want to do all this here, in your garden. Lupo's very much a part of the guest list, and they've spent all day staking out suitable locations. But of course,' she added hastily, 'I told them not to get excited until I'd spoken to you.'

He gave that oddly formal half-smile that turned her inside out. 'I think I could be persuaded,' he said drily, 'but I have an ulterior motive. There's something I need to ask you in return.'

*Oh, God,* she thought in a panic. *This is where he tells me he needs me to leave at the end of the week.* Her heart seemed to have lodged somewhere in the back of her throat.

'OK,' she said slightly breathlessly, 'but do you think we could go back up to the house? It's just that I don't really like leaving Lottie. I mean, I know she's asleep and we're not far away, but I just want to know that if she did wake up…'

And that if Sarah felt as though she was going to burst into tears she could make an excuse about getting dinner on or fetching a cardigan. And the temple, with its beautiful memories, would remain intact in her mind as the place where she'd known a few moments of perfect peace.

They walked back across the lawn. He was the one person who could make her feel delicate, she thought sadly; because he was so tall, and his shoulders so broad, but also because she felt protected by him. The evening sun turned the *palazzo* into an image from an ancient fresco, a vision of some earthly paradise, unchanged for five hundred years. It could not have brought home to her more forcefully what she was losing.

She gave a soft, wistful laugh. 'Lottie was right when she said it's the loveliest place on earth.'

'She was also right when she said it was far too big for one person.'

They had reached the courtyard now. Lorenzo put the glasses down on the antique table with its peeling paint and Sarah went inside to check on Lottie. Before going downstairs again she slipped into her bedroom and checked her reflection in the mirror, resisting the ridiculous urge to slap some make-up on her pink cheeks.

For what, exactly?

Lorenzo was sitting on the bench in the courtyard, staring moodily out over the garden. 'Everything all right?' he said as she came out again.

'Fine. She's asleep,' Sarah said, sitting down.

They might have been any couple discussing their child, Lorenzo thought with a wrenching sensation in the pit of his stomach. '*Bene,*' he said gruffly. 'Now, I've got something to ask you, but you must promise to say no if you want to.'

Fleetingly his mind flickered to the other question he had to ask her. About the film. Things were coming together so well that it alternately excited and terrified him. Very soon he could tell her all about it, but first he had to get this out of the way.

'That was Tia on the phone before,' he began carefully, turning his wine glass round in his fingers.

'I know.'

She was picking at the peeling paint on the table, but Lorenzo was too preoccupied to notice the note of misery in her voice. 'She was ringing to remind me about Venice. I hadn't forgotten, but I had managed to push it to the back of my mind—these things are to be endured rather than enjoyed at the best of times.'

'What things?'

'It's the film festival. *Circling the Sun* is being premiered, and she was making sure that I'd be there to witness her triumph.'

A patch of dirty grey paint was gradually being revealed beneath her nervous fingers. 'Triumph?'

He sighed. 'It's a media scrum. Obviously all the media interest will be firmly focused on her and Ricardo and my reaction to seeing them together, so the film itself will hardly get a mention. One-nil to Tia.'

'Are they still together?' she asked dully.

'Yes.' Aware of the savagery in his tone, Lorenzo took a mouthful of wine, as if that could wash it away. 'There's not much I can do to put the focus back on the film rather than the off-screen drama, but there's no doubt that much of the voyeuristic *frisson* will be taken out of the story if I don't turn up alone.' He set his wineglass down and thrust a hand through his hair. '*Dio,* Sarah, I'm not exactly selling this to you, am I?'

There was a pause. 'You're asking me to go with you?'

'*Si.* I know your track record when it comes to saying no, and the last thing I want to do is take advantage of you. I'll make it as brief and painless as poss—'

Relief made her too eager. 'OK. I mean, no, you don't have to do that. I'd be happy to come with you.'

'That was easier than I thought,' he said drily.

She took a large gulp of wine and nearly choked. 'Well, you're not the only one with an ex to score points from,' she said when she could speak again. 'It's not going to do any harm for Rupert to see me on the red carpet at the Venice Film Festival on the arm of a…top Italian film director, is it?' She was blushing more than ever now, partly because she always blushed when she lied, and saying Rupert was her reason for agreeing to this with such enthusiasm was a whopper. But mainly because she'd almost said 'sexy'. On the arm of a sexy Italian film director. 'He probably thinks I'm still sitting on the sofa in a grim flat in Shepherd's Bush, working my way steadily through boxes of tissues and packets of biscuits as I pine for him.'

'Well, he'll be in for a surprise,' Lorenzo said almost coldly. 'And there's no doubt that he will see you—the Press scrutiny is pretty harsh. You're ready for that? You don't need more time to think about this?'

She shook her head, but his words had sent a chill of uncertainty stealing down inside her. It wrapped its clammy fingers around her heart as she imagined banks of photographers lined up and pointing their long lenses at her like weapons.

'Do you? I mean, I'm not exactly red-carpet material.'

'You are,' he sighed. 'Don't worry about any of that.'

Warmth tingled inside her, deep inside her, as his unsmiling gaze moved lazily over her face, her cleavage in the unbuttoned V of her shirt. She gave him a weak smile. 'OK. Why would

I? By the end of this, fashion editors across the world will be hailing "housekeeper chic" as the new look, and journalists will be clamouring to discover the secret of my unique style and how I achieve my enviable "just got out of bed" hair.'

He laughed, but his eyes were serious. 'You're probably right. Rupert won't be able to get the ring off that poor woman's finger fast enough.'

# CHAPTER THIRTEEN

'I DON'T believe it. Why didn't you tell me you had a private plane?'

Sarah stopped just inside the doorway of the small Citation jet and turned to face him, her eyes round with amazement. Lorenzo smiled.

'I don't. It's only hired. I did promise I'd make this trip as quick and painless as possible. My excuse is that this is certainly the quickest way to do it.'

'And the most painless,' she laughed as a steward appeared with a bottle of champagne in an ice bucket.

'Would you like to take a seat, *signorina?*' said the steward. 'We will be ready for take-off in a few moments.'

'Can I have a look around first? Would you mind? I've never been on a private plane before. In fact, I've only ever been on a public one a few times, so all this is completely new. Oh, look—there's a little fridge, and a television. What does this button do?'

'It's a satellite communications system, *signorina.*'

Lorenzo watched, unable to quite suppress a smile at her excitement. God knew, he wouldn't have much to smile about over the next twenty-four hours, which promised to be about as much fun as root-canal work, but Sarah's sweetness and enthusiasm were like a shaft of sunlight in a darkened room. Tia would have been having a diva tantrum about the champagne not being the right kind, or the air-conditioning drying out her skin or something.

Sarah turned to him, her eyes shining with delight.

'Gosh—Lottie and Dino would love this.'

'You want to phone home?'

She hesitated and for a fraction of a second her face clouded. Then she flashed that quick, brave smile again and shook her head. 'And interrupt the camping fun? I don't think so. She probably hasn't even noticed I'm gone yet.'

'Are you OK?'

'Yes. Yes, of course.' She sat down on one of the squashy seats and stroked a hand over the gleaming beige leather. 'It's weird, that's all; I mean, I've hardly ever left her overnight before. But it's good. Really good that she's made a friend and got the chance to be a bit more independent. It's what I wanted and there just weren't the opportunities in London.'

Lorenzo sat down opposite her and took the champagne bottle from the bucket of ice. 'So, in spite of having to do this, you're not regretting your decision to stay?'

'No,' she laughed, taking the glass of champagne he handed her. 'And it's not much hardship to be doing this either.'

'Yet,' he said grimly. 'This is the easy part. Wait until later when you're standing in front of the bloodthirsty Press pack.'

The laughter faded from her lips and she looked at him seriously. 'Will it be that bad?'

'I'll make sure you're protected from the worst of it.'

His fingers tightened on his glass and for the hundredth time he wondered if he was making a huge mistake. A huge, selfish mistake.

He looked at her now, leaning forward to gaze out of the window as the plane started to move along the runway. Her plump lower lip was caught between her teeth, and the sun streaming through the window highlighted the freckles on her nose, and made gold and copper lights dance in her hair. After a month at Castellaccio she had lost her haunted look and her exceptional, clear skin was tanned to the colour of the froth on the top of a cappuccino. There was still that same nervous, self-effacing edge to her that he'd noticed the moment she'd walked into The Rose and Crown that night, but it was less pronounced now, so that the first thing you noticed about her was her air of quiet, almost slumberous sensuality.

That was the first thing *he* noticed about her, anyway, he thought acidly, draining half a glass of champagne in one mouthful.

The irony was that was exactly what he'd hoped for when he'd asked her to stay on at the *palazzo*. He'd wanted to take the ghosts from her eyes, and the anxious frown from beneath her brows. He'd wanted to make her see herself as attractive and special. But in order to do that, to make her stay, he'd promised to keep his distance.

If he'd known then how hard it would be, would he ever have been honourable enough to ask?

They were airborne now, the clouds spread below them in billowing layers of gossamer like Angelica's wedding veil, the sky above them an endless expanse of cerulean blue. Looking out of the window, Sarah was aware of him looking at her and hoped he wasn't already doubting the wisdom of bringing her. She wouldn't blame him. Was she the only person who had ever travelled by private jet wearing a faded old T-shirt that had shrunk in the wash and still bore the orange stain of a particularly good ragu sauce she'd made last week?

Not that it mattered much what clothes she travelled in, but the issue of what to wear tonight was much more problematic. She'd brought the lilac dress she'd worn to Angelica's wedding because it was the only possible option, but it was hardly the stuff of red-carpet glamour. She hoped she wouldn't let Lorenzo down. She'd thought about telling him that she had nothing to wear, but suspected that he'd then feel compelled to offer to buy her something, which would be horribly embarrassing.

He'd given her so much already.

\* \* \*

Sarah had thought the plane was impressive, but nothing could have prepared her for the hotel.

Briefly taking her hand as she stepped from the vaporetto, Lorenzo said, 'Most people going to the festival stay down in the Lido, but I prefer to be removed from the media circus as much as possible. This place is much more discreet.'

Inside the reception hallway it was cool and dim. Discreet probably wasn't the first word that would have occurred to her to describe such breathtaking grandeur, but she looked around at the vast, dark oil paintings in gilded frames a foot thick and impossibly ornate chandeliers as Lorenzo spoke to the concierge behind the desk and decided it was fitting. Everything wore a patina of age and there was nothing glossy or sleek or remotely high-tech about it, so that it felt a little like stepping out of the twenty-first century and through some secret doorway to the past…

'Ready?'

Lorenzo raised an enquiring eyebrow at her as he moved away from the desk. She hurried after him, her shamefully shabby flip-flops slapping on the marble floor.

'What time is the screening?' she asked as the lift doors slid shut, enclosing them together in dark-panelled intimacy. It was important to keep the conversation going, to drown out the thudding of her heart.

'Seven tonight,' he said curtly.

'Oh, but that's ages.' Surprised, she checked her watch. 'It's only just midday now. That means I've got loads of time to look around the city.'

He glanced at her with an expression of rueful amusement as the lift shuddered to a halt and the doors opened. 'I'm afraid not,' he said, striding along a corridor lined with marble statues of women in various stages of undress.

She frowned. 'Oh. Is there something we have to do first?'

He stopped in front of a set of huge double doors, and swiped the key card down the reader at the side. 'Not "we",' he said gently. 'You. Welcome to the world of the A-list celebrity.'

The doors opened, and Sarah felt her jaw drop. She was standing on the threshold of a huge square room with a wall of floor-to-ceiling windows overlooking the Grand Canal. After the gloom of the corridor the light shining on the polished marble floor and glinting on mirrors was almost dazzling, but it wasn't that that made her gape in astonishment, but the three portable metal clothes rails that stood in the centre of the room, shimmering with a rainbow of silks and satins.

Two effortlessly elegant women were standing by the window, their gazelle-like figures framed gorgeously by the view, so that they looked like a carefully posed photograph from Italian *Vogue*. Breaking off their conversation, they came forward, their catlike eyes flickering over Sarah appraisingly.

'Sarah, this is Natalia and Cristina. They're stylists. The dresses here have been donated by designers, and they'll help you to choose something that you like for tonight.'

Sarah looked anxiously at the rails of clothes and thought of the lilac dress in her bag. She could feel a scarlet tide of embarrassment creep up her neck. Tonight was obviously a bigger deal than she'd thought.

'O-OK,' she stammered, shaking one cool, elegant hand after the other. 'That's g-great, I think. When is everyone else getting here?'

'Well, the beautician will be arriving in the next couple of hours, when you've had time to decide what to wear. And the hair and make-up girls will come some time this afternoon.'

Sarah's mouth fell open in astonishment. 'But all these clothes can't be for me?' she said faintly. 'How will I ever choose?'

'That's what Natalia and Cristina are here for. Don't worry, everything is on loan, and they're under strict instructions not to pressure you into anything you hate. Don't let them bully you.'

Natalia and Cristina laughed politely as Lorenzo turned and walked back to the door. They were still looking at Sarah in a

way that was making her nervous, as if, like the Siamese cats
from one of Lottie's favourite Disney films, they were about to
pounce on her and eat her up the minute Lorenzo left.

'Where are you going?' she said, trying to keep the panic
from her voice.

'I have meetings lined up this afternoon. Sorry, but it's too
good an opportunity to miss while everyone is in town. I'll be
back to collect you about six.'

And with that he was gone.


Why, thought Sarah three hours later as she lay on the bed with
a pillow stuffed in her mouth, did perfectly sensible women put
themselves through this voluntarily?

She gave a muffled cry of pain as the beautician yanked
another wax strip from her right shin with brutal relish.
Stripping down to her awful chewing-gum-coloured underwear in front of Natalia and Cristina had been bad enough, but
the day had taken on a sinister Marquis de Sade-type aspect
since the arrival of the beauty team. Her face had already been
steamed and scrubbed and her eyebrows agonisingly twee-
zered until a surreptitious glance in the mirror confirmed she
looked every bit as battered and bruised as she felt.

And some women thought this was fun?

To Sarah it felt like the last stage of psychological endurance
training for some dangerous job as a top-level spy. Next they'd
probably be thrusting her head down the loo and demanding
that she give them names.

'Legs all done,' purred the beautician girl, delicately rubbing
wax from her fingers. 'Next I do your bikini line.'

'No!' squeaked Sarah, sitting bolt upright and clutching her
hotel bathrobe around her. The beautician looked disapprov-
ing, as if Sarah had just announced she didn't believe in
brushing her teeth.

'OK,' she sniffed. 'Nails?'

But in the end Sarah did have to admit that there was some

truth in the old saying that you had to suffer to be beautiful. When it was eventually time to shrug off the bathrobe and put on the underwear Natalia and Cristina had chosen for her, she was able to do it without a fraction of the self-consciousness she'd felt earlier, and for once she didn't avoid catching her own reflection in the mirror.

Not that it would have been possible anyway, since the room was virtually all mirrors, but the smooth, bronzed, gleaming body that she saw in them was barely recognisable as her own. With ceremonial reverence Natalia and Cristina stood on either side of her, helping her into the dress they'd all agreed on the moment Sarah had tried it on. It was made of heavy duchesse satin, the colour of raspberries crushed with a little cream, and its gloriously simple empire style was the perfect showcase for Sarah's cleavage, which they declared was '*magnifico*'. Although definitely not the kind of person to swoon over a pair of shoes, even Sarah had to admit that the cerise high-heeled sandals they had chosen to go with it, with ribbons that tied all the way up her legs, were extraordinary lovely.

But the source of her most profound joy was the magic wrought by the two hairdressers, who washed and massaged and anointed her disobedient curls with expensive-smelling serums before smoothing them between straightening irons with patient ruthlessness. Now her hair fell down past her shoulders like a curtain of heavy shot silk.

'*Bella. Se Bella,*' Natalia sighed in complete satisfaction as she stood back and surveyed the finished result, and murmurs of reverential agreement went around the rest of the assembled party. Looking in the mirror, Sarah felt an inner glow of happiness, which somehow seemed to radiate outwards. She might never be beautiful, but tonight was the closest she was ever going to get to it, and with that she was content.

The knock at the door broke the enchantment and suddenly the room was filled with a crackle of electricity. Natalia and Cristina went into a flurry of last-minute tweaks, smoothing a seam here, adjusting a strap there, before melting away with the rest of the girls into the suite's adjoining bedroom.

And then the door opened and he was there.

Sarah forgot to breathe.

He was dressed impeccably, but with just a touch of disdain in a plain black suit and black shirt open at the collar. He was cleanly shaven, his hair still damp from the shower. He looked arrogant, remote and faintly menacing as his dark gaze travelled over her.

And she saw it. A momentary flash of disappointment. She felt the split second's hesitation like the lash of a whip.

'You look beautiful,' he said gruffly, forcing a smile as his eyes met hers. 'Really. Very lovely.'

She picked up her little silver clutch bag. 'Shall we go?' Miraculously, she managed to produce a smile, determined that he shouldn't see that inside she had died a little.

Beautiful for her, maybe. But just not beautiful enough.

# CHAPTER FOURTEEN

LORENZO followed her along the corridor, unable to take his eyes off her perfect, rounded behind encased in raspberry-pink satin.

At least that was one thing about her that hadn't changed, he thought wearily.

He'd been telling the absolute truth. With her designer dress, her high heels, her lipgloss and mascara she looked absolutely sensational. But completely unfamiliar. It was the difference between a glorious, full-blown cottage-garden rose, exploding with scent, and the rigid, waxen, death-like perfection of the roses that came from expensive florists, presented in layers of cellophane.

He preferred the first, and he loathed himself for his own hypocrisy. He had done this to her—she hadn't asked for any of it, and he loathed himself for that even more.

They had reached the lift again. She got in ahead of him and pressed the button for the ground floor.

'Your nails,' he said softly. 'You have the nails you always wanted.'

They were a pale, glossy pink with delicate crescents of white at the tips, just as she'd described that time in Gennaro's.

She spread her hands out and looked down at them wistfully. 'I know. At last I'm a proper woman. If only Lottie were here to see it.'

*A proper woman. Dio santo.* He had a sudden image of her

in the kitchen, her hair tumbling messily around her face, her breasts straining against the faded green T-shirt as she bent to put something in the dishwasher, making her short denim skirt rise at the back to show more of her delicious legs… She was a proper woman through and through. A real woman. Not one of those dolls Lottie had described with such disdain.

The water taxi he had ordered was waiting at the hotel landing stage and he helped her in, catching a fleeting breath of her warm scent as he lowered himself in beside her.

'You smell nice.'

'Really?' Her neatly arched eyebrows rose in surprise. 'They tried to spray me with perfume but I said no. It must be the hair products or something.'

It wasn't. It was *her*.

The sun was setting over the water, and it was that hour when the city underwent its nightly transformation from crowded, noisy tourist magnet to subtle, secret city of lovers. The buildings along the Grand Canal were bathed in the dying light of the day, which flattered their faded beauty to perfection. The breeze made Sarah's straight, heavy hair fan out like the silken Venetian flags that topped so many buildings, rippling in the setting sun.

'Oh. I almost forgot. I picked this up on my way back.'

He took a flat box from his pocket and handed it to her, watching her face as she lifted the lid. Her mouth opened and her eyes widened, and despite the lipgloss and the mascara and shimmering eyeshadow she was herself again, her emotions still as clearly on display as ever as she lifted out the delicate web of silver wires and diamond stars.

'Lorenzo—it's incredible! It's the most beautiful thing I've ever seen. Are you sure it's OK for me to wear it?'

'I deliberately didn't give it to you in front of the style police back at the hotel in case they disapproved. But if you like it, wear it.'

'I do. I love it. Natalia said that they hadn't had time to

organise the loan of any jewellery—insurance or something—so did you sort all that out when you borrowed it? Apparently it's a bit of a legal nightmare.'

'Don't worry,' he said drily. 'It's all under control.' Because he hadn't borrowed it, he'd bought it, amongst other things, in a fit of temporary madness on the way back from his meeting with the very up-and-coming English actor whom he had asked to play the lead in the film of Francis Tate's book. Damian King had got a cult TV-drama series under his belt and was just finishing a very successful season at the RSC when his agent had given him a copy of *The Oak and the Cypress*. This afternoon he had been perfectly upfront and unstinting in his enthusiasm.

Buoyed up by champagne and elation, Lorenzo had gone into a discreet jewellery shop in a quiet *calle* and bought the necklace with its constellations of stars and the single moon hanging in the centre. There was a smaller version, for Lottie, and…

'Please can you put it on?'

Her sleek, heavy hair glinted gold and copper in the tangerine light of the sinking sun. A tremor of pure, powerful desire shook him as he swept it to one side, exposing the nape of her neck.

It was getting more difficult to ignore, this jagged, insistent wanting, he thought darkly. And it was now no longer possible to dismiss it as being motivated by some worthy intention to protect her and look after her best interests, or even the matter of the film rights. That was how it had started, admittedly, but at some point in between the kitchen and the temple, the oysters and the cake, it had gone beyond that into something far more debilitating and difficult to shake off.

'There.' He pulled his hands away as quickly as possible, clenching his fists against the urge to tangle his fingers in her hair and pull her head round so he could kiss off all that shiny pink lipgloss.

'Oh, Lorenzo, it's exquisite. You're so clever—I'd never

have picked anything as perfect as this. Gosh, wouldn't Lottie love it? I won't mind having my photograph taken so much now, because at least it'll mean she'll get to see it. Thank you.'

'No problem,' he said flatly, turning his head away and looking out into the lagoon as it opened up in front of them. Any excuse to avert his gaze from the stars glittering against her satiny skin, the little crescent moon nestling in the honey-coloured hollow between her glorious breasts. Otherwise the photographers would get some very incriminating photographs when he got out of the boat. 'Look, we're nearly there.'

Ahead, the glare of spotlights and the glitter of camera flashes lit up the gently fading evening. As they drew closer it was possible to see the great white wall of the screening venue, the rows of flags catching the gentle breeze above it, and hear the clamour of the crowd.

'There's the car waiting at the dock to collect us.'

She looked confused. 'Oh, yes. Is it far? I thought we were only going over there…'

'We are,' he said drily. 'But celebrities don't walk anywhere.'

The boat stopped and he stood up, holding out his hand to her. In spite of the unfamiliar make-up, the veneer of sophistication, her eyes wore that wide, wary look he had seen as soon as she'd walked into The Rose and Crown, and the lust of a second ago was almost obliterated by a wave of guilt.

He was about to throw her to the lions.

It was too late to turn back now. He'd just have to do what he could to make sure they savaged him first.

It was like one of those dreams where nothing made sense, and the most extravagantly bizarre things happened in the guise of normality. Sarah found herself getting into the car and perching on the shiny, slippery seat as beyond the darkened glass the night sparkled with thousands of camera flashes. And, like in a dream, she found it was the details that she noticed. The tiny letters on the window of the car that said 'bulletproof glass', the driver's white gloves, the muscle that was pulsing beneath Lorenzo's tense jaw.

Of course. In a few short moments he'd be coming face to face with the woman he loved, arm in arm with another man. No wonder he looked as if he was being silently tortured.

She longed to cover his hand with hers, and tell him she understood, but then the car was stopping in front of a wide building with a huge white frontage lit up with so many spotlights that it must surely be visible from the moon.

For a moment nothing happened, and then the door on Lorenzo's side was pulled smoothly open by unseen hands. In the half-second before he got out he looked at her with an expression of great weariness and said simply, 'I'm sorry.'

The noise hit her like a wall as she slid out of the car onto shaking legs. People shouting. Shouting his name—*Lorenzo*—but louder, more insistent, more fanatically, *'Tia! Ricardo!'* Camera flashes dazzled her, so brightly that she wanted to hide her head in her hands and run through them, like a sudden hail storm on the way to the Tube in Shepherd's Bush. But then Lorenzo took her arm and she ducked her head against the shelter of his massive shoulders.

'Look,' he murmured, bending his head and speaking close to her ear. 'Up there. In the sky.'

Cautiously she lifted her head and looked up, to where the pale ghost of the moon hung above them, gazing down on all the madness with her cool, impassive grace. Around them the clamour intensified. Very deliberately Lorenzo kept his eyes fixed on hers. 'The moon is looking down on Lottie too,' he said softly, so only she could hear. 'She's going to tell her how beautiful you are.' He smiled fleetingly. 'Especially your nails.'

Sarah laughed, and suddenly all the camera flashes and the spotlights put together were nothing to the light inside her. Keeping her head up, her fingers tightly laced through his, she let him guide her up the scarlet expanse towards the door of the theatre. He was very still, very upright, seemingly completely unmoved by the cheering crowd behind them, the banks of journalists to the right who shouted out his name in the hope of getting them to stop and pose for a shot or say a few words into one of the many microphones that were thrust forward. Glancing up at him, Sarah saw his face in the strobe-like flash of the cameras, and felt the glow of her happiness splutter and fade, as if the bulb she had swallowed had just gone out.

It was cold and bleak.

They were inside the mouth of the theatre entrance now, and the roar of the crowd echoed off the walls as Tia and Ricardo posed for more pictures. The sea of people who had pressed around Lorenzo and Sarah as they entered the enclosed space drew back, and suddenly there was no one between them and the other couple.

Nothing—not the airbrushed double-page spreads in life-style magazines, not the nude photoshoot that had caused such a stir, not the close-up camera angles in numerous films— could have prepared Sarah for how stunning Tia de Luca was in the flesh, and in that moment Sarah knew that all the make-up, the most expensive designer dresses and shoes in the world couldn't make her a millionth as lovely as the woman standing in front of her. In the glare of the spotlights her skin had a creamy luminosity, and her famous catlike eyes sparkled more intensely than the emeralds she wore at her throat and ears. She was, quite simply, very beautiful.

And very pregnant.

Oh, God, somehow, astonishingly, Sarah had forgotten that little detail. Lorenzo's fingers tightened convulsively around hers, and for a second she was distantly aware of the pain. But it was followed a moment later by a more acute hurt when he dropped her hand altogether.

'*Ciao,* Lorenzo.'

Her voice was like butter melting over crumpets: unctuous, slow, lascivious.

Lorenzo nodded. 'Tia. Ricardo.'

God, he was cool. Polite to the point of being almost insolent. Sarah was aware that every camera lens in the area was trained on them, and consciously tried to keep her misery from showing on her face. It was harder than it looked, this being-a-celebrity game, but Lorenzo and Tia and Ricardo were all masters.

'Aren't you going to introduce us?' Tia said, turning her megawatt smile from Lorenzo to Sarah.

'Sarah, this is Tia, my ex-wife, and Ricardo Marcello.'

Ricardo Marcello's handsome face was ridiculously familiar, but Sarah was completely unmoved by the legendary good looks. There was something bland and plastic about his bronzed skin and clichéd sculpted jaw, something anonymous about the straight nose and blue eyes that could make him be the face of any hero. Not like Lorenzo, who was all himself and infinitely more compelling.

'Sarah?' Tia cut through her thoughts. 'But surely we've spoken on the telephone, Sarah? You're Lorenzo's house-keeper?' The smile got wider, brighter, if that was possible. 'Oh, how lovely! You look so pretty—are you having a nice time? It's quite exciting, all this, isn't it?'

Tia turned, sweeping an elegant hand, flashing diamonds around at the Press and the crowd and the cameras. Sarah felt about two inches tall.

'Unreal is more how I'd describe it,' she said quietly.

Tia laughed, throwing back her head like in the photo in Gennaro's, and all around them the camera flashes glittered like fireworks.

'I'm afraid to us it's all *too* real, although Lorenzo has never enjoyed it, have you, *mio caro?* Ah, I think they want us over there for some photographs. I'm sure they won't mind if you come too, Sarah.'

As they stood in front of the ranks of photographers Sarah felt as if her lipglossed smile was superglued to her face. Lorenzo's arm was loosely around her, his hand warm on her bare shoulder, but in every other way it felt as though he was a million miles away.

'Are you coming to the Press conference tomorrow?' Tia asked as they moved away again, and into the screening room.

'No,' Lorenzo said tersely, and Tia looked put out.

'Really, Lorenzo, you have to face the Press at some point, you know. I know there are bound to be difficult questions,' she dropped her voice to a perfectly pitched husky murmur, 'but if we—'

'It has nothing to do with you, Tia,' Lorenzo said coldly. 'Sarah has a small daughter and we need to get back to her.'

They had come to a standstill in front of the row of VIP seats with their name cards on. All of a sudden the atmosphere seemed to change. For a second Tia went very still, and then quietly, venomously she said something in Italian that Sarah didn't understand.

'*Ipocrita.*'

As she said it her beautiful face was almost ugly.

The lights had gone up but the applause went on. And on. And on. Far longer than the film deserved. Lorenzo gritted his teeth in impatience as people in the rows behind leaned forward and slapped his back in congratulation, while Tia turned misty-eyed and waved to the cheering theatre.

Beside him, he was acutely aware of Sarah as she stretched slightly, blinking in the light and stifling a yawn. But then he'd been acutely aware of Sarah for the last two hours. It was funny, he thought. All those weeks of living under the same roof, and he'd managed to keep his distance and preserve the illusion that he was really not that attracted to her, but two hours sitting in the dark beside her, close enough to hear her breathing and to smell the warmth of her skin, to be aware of every tiny movement as she crossed her ankles, or smoothed back her hair, and he was like a lust-skewered teenager on a first date.

The film had passed him by completely, *grazie a Dio*.

The applause began to peter out and, desperate to seize the chance for escape, Lorenzo grabbed Sarah's hand.

'Come on. Let's get out of here.'

Before she could reply, Tia interrupted, 'You are coming to the party at the Excelsior, aren't you?'

'Absolutely not,' he said grimly, pulling Sarah after him as he made for the exit. 'Right,' he muttered as they reached the foyer, where the Press pack waited to engulf them again, 'hold your head up, smile like you've just had the best two hours of your life and walk quickly. The car will be waiting for us at the bottom of the steps. Everyone will assume we have somewhere very important to go.'

'And do we?'

'Yes.' He looked down at her briefly, desire churning inside him again. 'Away from here.'

They were the first out, and as they emerged the night was lit up with flashes again as a great shout went up from the gathered Press and public. Holding her hand very tightly, Lorenzo felt Sarah shiver as the cool air hit them, and he drew her quickly forward as PR girls and security men with headsets ran agitatedly up and down the cordons at the side of the red carpet.

After a moment he saw the reason for their sudden activity, and swore under his breath.

'The car's not there yet.'

Sarah's eyes widened as she looked up at him. The crowd were shouting his name. Journalists close by were calling out questions.

'What do we do?' she whispered.

'Stall. It'll be here in a moment.'

But from the crowd another shout came, clearly audible above the rest. *'Sarah! Over here, Sarah!'*

So it had taken the tabloid sharks just two hours to find out her name, Lorenzo thought with a surge of bitter fury. She was about to turn, instinctively ready to answer to her name and unwittingly surrender all her privacy, but he caught her, pulling her back and bringing his mouth down on hers.

A roar went up from the crowd and flashbulbs exploded like a meteor shower around them. Out of some inherent instinct to protect her, Lorenzo found himself taking her face between his hands, shielding it, preventing the cameras from getting a proper view of her like that.

Kissing him. Tenderly, hesitantly, tremulously, and with a quiet ferocity that left him breathless and reeling.

With mammoth effort of will he pulled away after a long, blissful moment, looking over her shoulder through a haze of debilitating desire to where the car was just pulling up in front of the steps.

'Let's go.'

# CHAPTER FIFTEEN

His face was like thunder as he slammed the car door and shut out the clamour of the crowd.

'Sorry. I shouldn't have done that.'

The chill in his voice made her wince. Shrinking back against the cold leather, she pressed her fingers to lips that still tingled from his kiss. 'Don't,' she said in anguish. 'Please. It's fine.'

He leaned back in his seat, his jaw set, his hands balled into fists. 'I didn't want them to put you on the spot. I never thought they'd find out so quickly who you are, and the last thing I wanted was for you to be put under the microscope. At least they won't be able to create too much of a story without any quotes to work with.' He stopped, rubbing a hand over his eyes for a second before continuing, 'I should never have exposed you to any of this.'

The car pulled up at the end of its short journey, but neither of them moved, and after all the frenetic noise the silence felt as soft and rich as fur. Sarah looked down into her lap, fiddling with the clasp of her handbag.

'I've told you,' she said quietly, 'I don't need protecting.'

Lorenzo was about to speak but the door opened, and they got out to walk the few steps down to the waiting water taxi. Darkness had fallen properly and the lights of the city made rippling trails of gold on the water. Behind them the disembodied screaming of the crowd rose into the night and echoed across the water and, looking back, Sarah could see a glowing arc of white light bleaching the skyline around the theatre. Ahead of them the moon was full and high, and it seemed to sail in front of them, leading them across the lagoon and back to…

*What?*

Sarah shivered.

'It's colder now,' Lorenzo said gruffly. 'Here,' and he slipped his jacket over her shoulders. Automatically, she demurred. 'No, honestly. I'm fine. I don't…'

'*Sarah, per piacere,* will you just let me do something for you for *once?*'

She stopped, her hands on the lapels of the jacket as the ragged despair in his voice tore through her. 'Sorry,' she whispered, pulling it closer around her, enfolding herself in the blissful borrowed warmth of his body. 'Sorry.'

Other boats passed them, dark shapes sliding past, bringing snatches of other people's conversation, other people's laughter. There was something spectral about the buildings on either side of the Grand Canal, floodlit from below so that their upper storeys faded into the night sky. Venice lay around them, its mysterious, ancient alleyways cloaked in darkness and silvered with moonlight, but after two hours in the cinema her head was still full of the dazzling colours and brilliant sunshine of Tuscany; a rich, sensual panorama of texture and detail that made her feel she could almost taste the wine from Galileo's cup, and smell the clean, earthy scent of cedar and lime in the air.

Lorenzo's smell, she thought with a sickening lurch of anguished yearning. He was in her, all around her, whether she liked it or not. She leaned on the side of the boat, letting the motion of the water rock through her as she gave herself up to reliving the moment when he'd kissed her. Oh, God, the ecstasy of having his hands on her face, his body pressed against hers. He'd probably been thinking of Tia, she thought despairingly. That would explain the sense of fierce, restrained passion she'd sensed in him, as if he was fighting with everything in him to keep control. He was fired up and torn apart by watching her on the screen.

The steps to the hotel landing stage loomed in front of them. Although she braced herself for the jolt when the boat hit the dock she still stumbled a little on the impossible heels, and instantly his arm was around her.

'Bene?'

'Yes,' she said breathlessly, forcing herself to step away from him immediately and take the hand of the hotel porter on the steps.

The hotel's reception area was softly lit and welcoming as they walked through it, Sarah's heels echoing on the marble floor. As they waited for the lift she slipped Lorenzo's jacket off her shoulders and handed it back to him.

'Thank you for lending it to me.' She gave a soft, breathy laugh. 'I feel like Cinderella—now I have to return all my borrowed finery and turn back into a kitchen maid.'

Lorenzo didn't smile. The lift doors shut behind them.

'The film was spectacular,' she said quickly, to try and break the sudden tension. 'Sorry, I should have said before. The moon sequences especially—Lottie would adore those—but all of it was brilliant. I loved it.'

Everything about him was as cold and upright and emotionless as the marble pillars they had just walked past in the reception area. 'At least that makes one of us then,' he said acidly. 'I hated every second.'

Sarah felt her insides constrict with compassion and longing. 'That's understandable,' she whispered. 'It must be very difficult to watch.'

'It's bloody excruciating,' he said through gritted teeth.

The lift stopped. Sarah nodded, biting her lip in anguish as she waited for the doors to open so she could step away from him and hopefully lessen the screaming urge to put her arms around his rigid shoulders. She pushed through the doors before they were even properly open, hurrying back along the corridor towards her room.

She didn't have the key, and stood at the huge double doors waiting for him, keeping her head down because she knew that if she watched him come towards her she would be completely undone.

The card was in his hand, but he didn't put it into the reader straight away. Sparks erupted inside Sarah's stomach as he gently took her chin in her hands and raised her face so she was looking up at him.

'Not because of Tia,' he said gruffly, 'in case that's what you think. I don't give a damn about her at all. That's not why I hate the film.'

For a second she couldn't breathe. The world blurred and stars danced in her head. 'Then why?'

He laughed softly. 'Because it's cliché-ridden, predictable, plastic Hollywood rubbish, that's why. And I *never* want to sell out by making a film like that again.'

He didn't let her go. He was frowning, almost as if he was in pain as his eyes burned into hers with that peculiar intensity that made her feel as if he was looking into her head, almost willing her to understand something.

'But I thought…' She swallowed. 'Tia—you're still in love with her?'

He laughed hollowly, shaking his head. 'No. *Dio santo,* no. I couldn't get the divorce through fast enough.'

Along the corridor the lift doors opened again and the sound of voices made them both jump. Lorenzo let her go, turning and sliding the key into the slot quickly. Sarah pushed the doors open, saying shakily over her shoulder, 'Would you like to come in for coffee or something?'

'No.'

Disappointment lacerated her at the thought of him going back to his own room, but was quickly followed by relief as he shut the door behind him and headed for an ornate, inlaid cabinet. 'I need a proper drink.'

The rails of dresses and mountains of shoe boxes had all

been removed, and the huge suite was intimidatingly immaculate again. The lights had been left on in the bedroom, and through the open door Sarah could see the sheets had been turned down on the enormous bed with its carved gold headboard. Suddenly light-headed with want, she went over to the window seat and sat down, raising up her skirt to untie the ribbons on her shoes and ease her aching feet out of them.

Thoughts seemed to be whirling around in her brain, but too fast to allow her to make any sense of them, so that it was like trying to look at the scenery through the window of a speeding train. When she looked up again Lorenzo was standing in front of her, holding a bottle of brandy and two glasses, his dark eyes hooded and opaque.

She took a glass from him, holding it against her chest as if it could warm her. The only thing she could focus on with any clarity was what Lorenzo had said about Tia. About not loving Tia. But how this was possible and what it meant was part of the blur.

'She said something to you, just before the film started. What was it?'

He took a mouthful of brandy. She watched his bronzed throat move as he swallowed.

'She called me a hypocrite.'

Sarah frowned. 'Why?'

'Doesn't matter,' he said, but the steel in his tone confirmed what she already suspected.

'It was something to do with me. Me and Lottie, wasn't it? I don't need protecting, Lorenzo. I'd like to know what she meant.'

He sighed, moving across so that he was standing in front of the window. In profile his face was harsh, uncompromising, arrogant. 'Obviously she assumed we're together. A couple.'

'And why would that make you a hypocrite?' Sarah's heart was thudding, a sensation of nameless dread creeping around her, as if ghostly faces with hostile eyes were peering at them through the blank, dark windows. 'You're divorced. You've both moved on.'

'Because you have a daughter.' He swirled the brandy around in his glass. 'And I left her because I wasn't prepared to be a father to Ricardo Marcello's child.'

Cautiously she took a sip of brandy. She didn't usually like it, but now she welcomed the burn at the back of her throat, which sharpened her senses a little, made her more able to think, and focus.

'But I thought she left you, for Ricardo,' Sarah's whirling mind swung dizzily back to the morning after the flood and the magazine in Angelica's kitchen, 'and that the baby was yours…'

His smile was chillingly bleak. 'Tia's very clever. As far as I know she hasn't said directly that the baby's mine but she's very carefully left her options open. It was me who asked for the divorce, but now she wants to come back. I think she's realising how much she liked being married to a director—it gave her a certain amount of status in the industry, and there's no room for two egos the size of hers and Ricardo's in one relationship.'

'Would you take her back?' Sarah forced the words through numb lips. 'If the baby was yours?'

'It isn't.'

Something in the way he said it made her put down her glass and get to her feet. Standing behind him, she could see his face reflected imperfectly in the glass of the window. His eyes were dark whirlpools.

'How? How do you know?'

The question came from her almost involuntarily. Part of her didn't want to know; wanted to retreat respectfully from the wound that she sensed lay beneath the terrifyingly controlled façade. But the other part of her knew she didn't have a choice—that, whatever it was and whatever had caused it, she had to share his suffering.

He took a mouthful of brandy, draining the glass.

'Because I can't have children. I'm infertile. Completely and irrevocably. So, you see, it would be a miracle if the baby was mine.'

The ormolu clock on the mantelpiece ticked on, as the aching bitterness of his words died in the quiet room.

Sarah said nothing. There wasn't anything she could say that wouldn't seem to diminish his hurt, so instead she slid her hands across his rigid shoulders, laying her cheek against them and pulling him close as a spasm of irrational loss and longing gripped her. This was the beating heart at the centre of his pain, she thought. Not being without Tia, but without children.

For a moment he didn't move, and then she felt his hand close around hers.

They stood like that for a long moment, and then gently, almost reluctantly, he pulled her round so that she was standing in front of him. Sarah sensed him hesitate, still caged by his own demons, and the realisation touched her unbearably and gave her strength. She couldn't take his pain away, but she could show him that she wasn't afraid of it. Reaching up, she took his face between her hands and raised herself up on tiptoe so she could kiss his mouth.

It was iron-hard with tension, and as her lips very gently moved across his she remembered the night in The Rose and Crown when he'd first kissed her and she'd been too shocked, too scared, too inhibited and insecure to respond. She remembered his tenderness, his patience...his smile, that in her paranoia and self-doubt she'd thought meant he was laughing at her. But now she understood that maybe, just maybe he'd been feeling a fraction of the helpless *rightness* she was feeling now. Her fingers slid into his silken hair, and she pressed soft kisses to the corner of his mouth and along the line of his jaw, until she felt the tautness leave it and heard him give a low moan.

'Sarah... *Dio,* I've tried to resist this for so long, but I don't think I can hold back any more.'

'Thank God for that.' She'd reached his ear, and broke off kissing to take the lobe in her mouth. 'If you did I think I'd die.'

A shudder of desire went through him and he wrenched his head round to capture her mouth with his. And suddenly everything was different. The kisses that they'd shared before—those tentative, desperate, forbidden kisses—had been like the disjointed strains of a solo violin, compared to the full orchestral symphony of this one. Sarah's body was on fire from inside, flames licking through her, spreading heat to her limbs and melting her so that she was dripping with longing and anticipation.

And she gave herself up to the blaze; arching herself against him as he held her and kissed so deeply it was as if he was looking for her soul. Her hands fumbled blindly at the buttons of his shirt, desire making her clumsy and uncoordinated. Unlike Lorenzo. Taking hold of her dress, he yanked up the heavy satin skirt in one swift tug, hitching it up and freeing her legs so that he could pick her up. Instinctively wrapping her legs around his waist, Sarah's fingers clenched and flexed and the first tremors of helpless ecstasy quivered through her as he pulled her hard against him and carried her into the bedroom.

He lowered her down onto the bed, but she kept her legs tightly clasped around him, pulling him down with her. As she grappled with his belt and the button of his trousers her mouth never left his. He tasted cleanly of brandy, and she drank him in with a desperate, urgent thirst, until at last his impatient fingers tangled with hers, swiftly, expertly tearing open his trousers, and Sarah tipped back her head and gave a triumphant cry of joy as she felt his erection against her parted thighs.

Time slowed, their breathing caught and faltered as he slid her silken knickers down and she looked up into his face with eyes that were unfocused with desire. She felt disorientated with need...and the finger he languidly stroked through her swollen folds pushed her closer to the edge. Helplessly she writhed against his hand, her mouth opening in a breathless gasp as paradise opened up before her.

With faultless timing, Lorenzo grasped her hips and thrust into her, his teeth clenched with the effort of not erupting inside her as her slippery heat gripped him and her hips rose up to meet him. But, gazing down at her face, her cheeks flushed, her eyes black and glittering with passion, he felt his control crack, and, as her muscles tightened convulsively around him and her crimson lips parted in a cry of pure joy, it shattered completely.

Dazed, exhausted, breathless, he lay in the ruins of his self-restraint and she in the wreckage of a three-thousand-pound, borrowed dress of raspberry satin. But as he gathered her into his arms in a ridiculously ornate bed Lorenzo Cavalleri felt almost at peace.

'Oh, God, Lorenzo.'

He lifted his head, the note of anxiety in her voice making his heart crash against his ribs and jerking him from his semi-somnolent state of bliss.

'What?' He looked down into her face, brushing a damp strand of hair from her cheek. 'Sarah, what's wrong?'

'The dress,' she whispered, rolling away from him and standing up unsteadily. 'How could I have forgotten about the dress? It cost a f—'

In a flash he was behind her, taking her in his arms, rocking her gently as he pressed kisses against the warm, bare skin of her shoulders. 'Shh—'

'But it's got to go back to the designer first thing tomorrow. Oh, God, I'm so stupid, I don't deserve such beautiful things.'

'You do, *assolutemente*. The dress isn't going anywhere, and neither is the necklace, although I have to agree it would be a lot better if we took them off now...'

'Lorenzo, no!' she said, horrified. 'I couldn't keep them. No way. Don't even *think* about it.'

'Well, I don't think the designer is going to want this back now,' he said slowly sliding down the zip of the dress and turning her around to face him as he pushed it from her shoulders, 'and the necklace was always yours to keep, so there's no point in arguing.'

The dress fell to the floor with a sigh. She wasn't wearing

a bra and Lorenzo felt his head rock back as he took in the full impact of her beautiful naked body.

'*Seraphina…*'

She bent her head, letting her hair fall over her face as she crossed her arms across her breasts. Her spectacular, generous, gorgeous breasts with their blush-pink nipples, and the diamond stars and moon glittering against her velvet skin. Very gently, he took her hands and pulled them away from her body.

He sensed her resistance. 'Don't, please…'

He took her face in his hands, stroking her cheeks with his thumbs. 'Sarah, you're exquisite,' he said gravely. '*Dio,* I knew you would be, but you're lovely beyond even my wildest, most X-rated dreams.'

'I'm not. I'm—'

She squealed as he swept her into his arms and hitched her against his chest, carrying her effortlessly into the bathroom, where he turned the shower on.

'You are, which accounts for my complete lack of finesse back there. You're impossibly beautiful—although I have to admit I much prefer you without make-up and with your glorious hair how it's supposed to be.' She gasped again as he set her down under the steaming jet of water and stepped in beside her, stopping any further chance of argument with his mouth on hers as the mascara ran down her cheeks.

Her face was clean of every last trace of make-up and her hair plastered to her head when he finally turned off the water and reached for a towel to wrap around her.

'Not Seraphina any more,' she said with a sad, shy smile. 'I'm Sarah again now.'

'You're always Seraphina,' Lorenzo growled, gently wiping the water from her face with the edge of the towel. 'You're beautiful through and through.'

The idea of taking her standing up in the shower held considerable appeal, but he had something altogether slower and more considered in mind as he led her back to the bedroom.

He had all night to show her how beautiful she was. Slowly, worshipping her goddess-like body inch by inch, with the reverence it deserved this time. He wanted to make her feel as good as she'd made him feel. Slay her demons as she'd slain his, with her understanding and her compassion and her generous, intuitive acceptance of his secret flaw.

He didn't intend to waste a moment.

# CHAPTER SIXTEEN

WAKING from a brief, disorientatingly deep sleep with the feel of Lorenzo's arm lying along her thigh, his legs tangled with hers, Sarah thought she was still dreaming. But then her eyes fluttered open and the opulent room took shape around her in the tentative grey light of early dawn, the room-service meal they'd shared at some time in the small hours, the empty bottle of champagne, and she smiled because she knew that every spine-tingling, blush-making detail was true.

Lorenzo's hand slid lazily up her thigh and he raised his head to kiss her mouth.

'*Buongiorno, bella.*'

His voice was husky and intimate with sleep and his black hair was tousled. In the half-light with the sheet barely covering him he looked absurdly young somehow, and as she leaned over and kissed him back Sarah realised it was because all the tension had left his face. She propped herself on one elbow, looking down on his body, taking deep pleasure from letting her gaze wander over his broad, powerful chest as it slowly rose and fell with each breath. His olive skin looked dark against the white sheets, and she trailed a finger down over the bumps of his ribs, remembering the first time she'd seen him without his shirt on, when he'd carried Lottie to bed that night. He'd been too thin then, but now the angles of his bones were less sharp, and she felt a deep-down, visceral sense of satisfaction that it was because of her. Her cooking, her care.

His lips twitched as her finger moved lower, and his gaze locked with hers. Sitting up, Sarah bit down on her lower lip, trying to suppress a wicked, delicious smile as she climbed on top of him and watched the darkness in his eyes deepen.

'I think I owe you a Screaming Orgasm,' she murmured as she bent her head and slid downwards.

The sky in the east was faintly tinged with pink, but the city still slept around them, its towers and domes wreathed in pearly grey mist. They were sitting on the balcony overlooking the canal, drowsy and replete, the doors behind them open and the magnificent bed in total disarray. Sarah was loosely wrapped in the satin coverlet from the bed, the diamonds glittering at her throat, her hair tumbling down about her naked shoulders and her legs tucked up in front of her as she sipped tea from a delicate china cup.

'You look like some wanton eighteenth-century duchess after a night of passion with Casanova,' Lorenzo said huskily.

She smiled at him over the rim of her cup, the steam wreathing her face. 'I feel like one. But Casanova would have been very put out to find he had a rival for the title of world's greatest lover. He probably would have challenged you to a duel on the Rialto or something.'

'The way I feel at the moment I would have taken him on,' he said drily. Tia had always made him feel as if his infertility was a weakness. It was her unspoken justification for flirting with other men, kissing them, sleeping with them, as if she was punishing him for being less of a man.

Tentative fingers of light stretched over the lagoon, and gradually the smudged silhouettes of buildings emerged from the shadows and were washed with pink and gold. Like Sarah, Lorenzo thought, coming forward into the light. In the new light her clear, clean skin was the pale rose-gold of the inside of a seashell. *Dio,* how could he ever make her see how incredible she was?

Last night he had made a start, but there was so much he still wanted to do…

He had almost said something about the film last night, when they had talked about *Circling the Sun.* He had so nearly told her about the kind of film he longed to make, but the atmosphere between them had been so highly charged that he hadn't been able to think straight. Hadn't wanted to break that sensual spell.

Hadn't wanted to risk her retreating from him again.

But he would do it soon. He had set up a meeting with distributors and studio bosses in London later in the week, but yesterday's coup with securing the lead actor made it almost just a formality. He didn't need financial backing…

All he needed now were the options rights. From Sarah.

But he didn't just want to ask her outright. This was about more than just the film now. This was about Sarah, and he wasn't just selling her the film, he was selling her Francis Tate. He was presenting to her a perspective on the past that might just change the way she saw the brilliant, troubled poet that Lorenzo had admired for so long, but who had left such scars on his own small daughter. And then she might just change the way she saw herself.

He had to make sure he handled it properly.

'Come along, Duchess.'

Getting to his feet, he held out his hand to her and gently pulled her up. The satin coverlet slid to the floor, so that she was standing naked in front of him, the new sun bathing her in apricot light.

'Where are we going?'

'The most attractive answer to that would be "back to bed",' he said ruefully. 'But there isn't time. You want to get back to Lottie, and I want to show you some of Venice before we go, and if I took you back to bed I might have to keep you there for the rest of the day.'

'Hmm…that sounds good.' Her voice was wistful, almost pleading. She placed the palms of her hands on his bare chest, and Lorenzo felt an instant, debilitating leap of desire. 'I'm sure Lottie's having the time of her life; we don't need to rush back…'

Gently he removed her hands and, taking hold of her shoulders, he drew her to him. 'We'll still have this when we get back to the *palazzo,* you know,' he said gruffly, kissing the top of her head, briefly breathing in the scent of her warm hair. 'I have to go to London on Wednesday, but when I get back we have all the time in the world.'

Sarah pulled away, hating herself for the sudden desolation she felt at the thought of leaving this enchantment and getting back to reality. Of him going away.

'You're going to London?' She said it slightly incredulously, as if she was surprised to hear that London still existed.

'*Si.*' He bent to pick up the satin coverlet and wrapped it around her, holding it tightly under her chin. 'For a day or two, that's all. I'll be back in time for Lottie's birthday on Sunday.'

Sarah laughed, torn between amusement and huge embarrassment. 'Oh, dear, she told you about that?'

'Only about fifty times. I've promised her a special treat.'

'Lorenzo, no!' she said quickly. 'You don't have to—'

'I *want* to,' he interrupted her calmly. 'Anyway, it's too late. It's all organised now, so there's no point in arguing. You'll be all right on your own at Castellaccio for a couple of days?'

'I'm used to being on my own, remember?' She ducked her head, pulling the satin wrap more tightly around herself, mumbling, 'But I'll miss you.'

'I wish I didn't have to go, but I do.' He sighed, and there was an odd note in his voice that was somewhere between wistfulness and determination. 'It's about the film project I'm trying to get off the ground.'

She raised her head. In the pale golden morning his haughty, high-cheekboned face was strangely vulnerable. Her heart clenched. 'It's important to you, this film, isn't it?'

He gave a painful smile. 'It's the most important thing I've ever done.'

The alleyways and squares were still echoing and empty as they walked through them wrapped in each other's arms. In that deserted dawn the city was so breathtaking that Sarah couldn't regret forgoing more basic pleasures for this one.

The plump pink sun turned the opaque greenish water of the canals into rivers of rosy gold and the bells of the many churches echoed out at intervals over the quiet, shimmering city. They passed a baker's, not yet open, but from which the scent of almonds and warm bread drifted enticingly, and which was happy to sell them hot croissants and fat, pale green cookies studded with pistachios to take home to Lottie and Dino.

Emerging again into the damp, cool morning, they walked back through St Mark's Square, empty but for a couple of waiters sweeping up and desultorily setting out chairs. The Basilica looked as if it were made from Turkish delight in the pink morning light. Lorenzo's arm was around her shoulders, his body big and hard and warm against hers, and he said, 'Later this will be so full of tourists that you won't be able to see the ground.' He pulled away from her, taking her hand and swinging her around until she was dizzy and laughing. 'But now it's yours. All yours,' he said, and then he drew her back into his arms and kissed her. And Sarah was so happy that she almost believed him.

They were both quiet on the flight back to Pisa, and as the car wound its way through the verdant Tuscan hills and ochre villages back to Castellaccio Sarah felt her happiness dim a little, as if a cloud had come over the sun. She was desperate to see Lottie, and deeply touched and grateful that Lorenzo had understood this morning how she needed to get back to her as soon as possible, but as they sped through the sun-baked green and gold of Tuscany, Venice in the diaphanous light of dawn seemed as insubstantial as a dream.

Beside her, Lorenzo steered the car effortlessly around alarming hairpin bends, one hand resting on her knee. But already he seemed remote and unreachable, lost in his own thoughts. She longed to ask him what they were, but didn't dare. He had said that it wouldn't be over when they got back to the *palazzo,* but somehow, no matter how she tried, she couldn't imagine them picking up where they had left off this morning once they were back there. In Venice she had become a different person: the kind of woman who wore designer dresses and had a team of experts to get her ready. The kind of woman who made passionate, uninhibited love in lavish hotel suites. Now she was bare-faced and back in her scruffy supermarket clothes, ready to return to being a mother. A housekeeper.

How could he possibly find her attractive with her arms full of washing, she thought sadly, the smell of cooking in her hair? Last night had given her a glimpse into his life, and the film had given her an insight into his phenomenal creativity and skill. His talent and vision and brilliance. How could an ordinary girl like her interest a man like that?

All the doubts were temporarily pushed to the back of her mind when they pulled into the drive of the *palazzo.* Lottie and Dino had been waiting by the gates with Lupo, and they all ran alongside the car, Lupo galloping madly at the children's heels as Lorenzo pretended to race them. He let them win, of course, and Sarah got out to greet them as they jumped up and down in victory by the front steps to the house.

She hugged Lottie close, breathing her in.

'Did you have a good time?' she asked as Paola appeared, smiling and drying her hands on a tea towel.

'Oh, *yes,*' Lottie cried, her eyes shining. 'We ate hot dogs and *gelato* and Alfredo played the guitar and taught me an Italian song, and we stayed up until it was really late and there was a *full moon,* and it was huge, so it didn't really get dark and the garden was all silvery, and Lupo slept in our tent...' She broke off for breath, then shrugged and said simply, 'I had the best time *ever.* Did you?'

'Yes,' Sarah said quietly, catching Lorenzo's eye for a dizzying moment. 'I saw the moon as well. In Venice, shining on the water. And I missed you, but I had the best time too.'

Paola and Alfredo stayed for supper. Sarah made a very simple dish of tagliatelle with pesto and they all sat out in the courtyard until dusk had fallen and the children's heads were drooping with tiredness.

After they'd gone, in a flurry of *arrivedercis* and *grazies,* Lorenzo hoisted a half-asleep Lottie into his arms and carried her upstairs to her little room with the starry ceiling. Following a moment later, Sarah stood at the doorway watching him as he laid her gently in bed. She said something to him that Sarah didn't hear, and he smiled, stroking her hair back from her forehead, but as he straightened up again his face wore an expression that was almost like pain.

She remembered the bleakness in his voice when he'd told her last night that he couldn't have children of his own, and her heart ached. She longed to say something to him—to reach out to him and reassure him—but when she had said goodnight to Lottie and came out of the room there was no chance to say anything as he took her hand and led her through the summer twilight to his room. They undressed each other with trembling, tender urgency and she could only show him what she couldn't say in words.

The edges of the room had retreated into blurry darkness as she lay in his arms afterwards, her body still pulsing and wracked with pleasure. She could hear his heart beating beneath her cheek, steady and reassuring, and felt the gentle rise and fall of his chest as he breathed.

Emotion swelled and hardened in the back of her throat, stopping her breath and making her dizzy. She suddenly felt as if the world was spinning, faster and faster, and that there was nothing to stop her from being flung off and falling, spinning, hurtling down into nothingness.

Just as she had fallen in love with him.

She hadn't meant it to happen, but in the end she was as powerless to stop it as gravity. And she stuffed her knuckles in her mouth and prayed that she wouldn't wake him up with her stupid, irrational crying. Because then he would ask her what the matter was and she'd have to tell him that she was happy. That she was so happy that it scared her.

In the few brief, sunlit days that followed Sarah felt as if she was living in a bubble; one of the delicate, iridescent bubbles that Lottie blew through a wand, which wavered and shimmered over the lawn before vanishing in a shower of rainbow droplets.

She and Lorenzo made love in the early mornings, in the tranquil hour before dawn when the air was cool on her skin; and in the sultry purple dusk, when Lottie was asleep. They would come together on the stairs, in the garden, on the chill tiles of the kitchen floor, satisfying their craving for each other quickly and hungrily, before falling into bed and doing it all over again. Slowly and luxuriously.

On Wednesday morning she woke early, twisting gently from the circle of his arms so she could turn and look at his face as he slept. The dewy light made his dark skin look unnaturally pale. Asleep, he seemed to inhabit somewhere completely beyond her reach, and she wondered what dreams were playing across his brilliant, endlessly fascinating mind.

In spite of the warmth of his body next to hers she felt suddenly cold and regretted moving out of his embrace. But then his thick, dark lashes fluttered and his mouth widened into a slow, sleepy, unmistakably sexy smile.

'I was just dreaming about you,' he said huskily, pulling her against him.

There was something more intense in their lovemaking that morning, something that touched her more profoundly even than before, when he'd taken her so high that she felt as if she was soaring with the angels. But this time there was no sense of blissful abandon. Lorenzo leaned over her, his dark, compelling gaze never leaving hers as he filled her, slowly and deeply, and it felt as if he was saying goodbye.

*I'm being completely ridiculous,* she told herself sternly, clattering crockery in the kitchen as Lottie's bright chatter filled the silent spaces that lay over the breakfast table. Lorenzo listened patiently, smiling enigmatically as she tried to extract clues from him about the birthday treat he had promised, while Sarah busied herself clearing plates and giving herself a strict talking-to.

What happened to the girl who used to pride herself on her independence? she thought disgustedly, tossing her untouched toast to a grateful Lupo. Weeks had used to go by without her hearing a word from Rupert, and she barely gave it a thought.

But then she hadn't loved Rupert.

Not as she loved Lorenzo.

He wouldn't let her drive him to the airport, so they said goodbye in the bright sunshine outside the *palazzo*. Throwing his bags into the car, he bent down to give Lottie a hug.

'*Arrivederci, tesoro. A presto.*'

'*A presto, Lorenzo,*' she said in a small voice. 'Why do you have to go?'

'Because I have some work to do.' He smiled. 'And because I have some arrangements to make for a certain someone's birthday treat.'

She threw herself into his arms, and Sarah had to turn away as Lorenzo stroked her hair and said, 'Look after Lupo for me. And your *mama.*' God, she wasn't going to cry, that would be too pathetic for words, but seeing her little girl enfolded in Lorenzo's huge arms was almost too much.

He set Lottie down and stood up, taking her hand and pulling her towards him. Since their return from Venice by some unspoken mutual agreement they'd kept the shift in their relationship secret, making sure Lottie didn't have any reason to suspect that anything had changed. Now, gripping her hand tightly, he looked straight into her eyes.

'*Mi mancheri.*'

She laughed, because it was better than crying. 'Why can't my Italian be as good as Lottie's?'

'I'll miss you. But I'll be back very soon.' Clenching his teeth, he turned his head away so she could see the muscle flickering in his cheek, and the shadowy anxiety that had been stealthily stalking her for the past few days closed in on her a little.

'Lorenzo?' she whispered.

But whatever it was she had seen on his face had passed, and he turned back and kissed her hard, on the mouth, while Lottie looked on, her eyes as round as saucers. And then he got into the car and drove off quickly, the tyres throwing up clouds of dust from the drive.

The big old house felt very empty without him. It wasn't the only one, Sarah thought with a sigh as she trailed through the hallway with a basketful of washing. He'd only been away for—she glanced at the huge old grandfather clock beside his study door, and frowned. An hour? It felt like much longer.

And then she gave a shaky laugh as she noticed that the clock had stopped. Of course it was more—three hours at least—but without him she felt pretty much like the clock. Stopped. Waiting.

Beyond pathetic, she thought with a disdainful sniff, hitching the washing basket up on her hip and heading for the stairs with renewed purpose.

She was stopped in her tracks by the ring of the telephone. Dropping the basket at the bottom of the stairs, she ran across the hall and into Lorenzo's study to answer it, her pulse quickening at the thought that it might be him. Would he be there yet? In London? Perhaps he was ringing to tell her he'd just landed…

'Hello?'

'Oh, hi,' said a voice on the other end. English, female and surprised. 'I was bracing myself to struggle with my basic Italian, but you're English, right?'

'Yes,' said Sarah, choking back her disappointment.

'Great, that makes it easier. Are you Mr Cavalleri's PA, by any chance?'

Through the open door Sarah could see the washing spilling out of the basket onto the hall floor. 'I work for Mr Cavalleri, yes,' she said wryly. 'I'm afraid he's not here at the moment.'

'No, I know that,' the girl said easily. 'I'm Lisa, Jim Sheldon's PA. Jim's got a meeting with Mr Cavalleri later on this afternoon, so he's gone to check out the location for the project and he's just phoned in to say he's lost. Honestly, it's typical. Mr Cavalleri's not answering his phone, so I assume he's still in the air, and I've got Jim calling me on his mobile from the middle of darkest Oxfordshire having a complete meltdown. I just wondered if you could help me point him in the right direction.'

'Oh,' said Sarah, faintly. Her pulse was drumming so loudly in her head she had to press the phone very hard against her ear to hear the breezy cockney voice at the other end. 'Oxfordshire. Right. I'll do my best. Where is he heading for?'

There was the sound of papers rustling at the other end and Lisa's voice was distracted. 'Um...well, I gave him directions to the village, but now apparently he's looking for some pub or other. Mr Cavalleri said it was important in the book...'

Sarah lowered herself abruptly into the chair in front of Lorenzo's desk. She was finding it hard to breathe, and her legs felt suddenly bloodless.

'What book?'

'Oh, sorry.' Lisa, whoever she was, sounded surprised. 'Jim's talked about nothing else for weeks, so I assumed it would be the same at your end. *The Oak and—*'

'*The Cypress,*' Sarah finished hoarsely. Dark spots danced in front of her eyes.

'That's the one. Jim's so excited about it, especially since

Damian King's on board now. All very hush-hush, of course, but we've just got to keep our fingers crossed that Mr Cavalleri manages to pull off all the legal stuff. Anyway, the pub—do you know what it's called?'

'The Rose and Crown.' Sarah's swollen throat ached with the effort of sounding normal. 'It's off the main road, about a mile or so outside Lower Prior on the road to Stokehampton.' *Or less, if you cut through the fields…*

'Oh, that's brilliant. Thanks so much. I'll phone him back now and…'

Sarah didn't listen to the rest. The phone had slipped down onto her shoulder and she held it there for a while, staring straight in front of her as her mind inched slowly back over the last month, blindly groping over everything that had happened and suddenly understanding.

Why he'd taken such an interest in her. Why he'd asked her to stay on, and why he'd taken her to Venice and bought her the necklace and…and…seduced her so very, *very* thoroughly. Oh, God. It must have been him who had applied for the rights to the book. And after she had refused he had set out to do all he could to guarantee success…

*'No!'* The cry of anguished denial was torn from her and she jumped to her feet, dropping the phone back into its cradle with a clatter before yanking open the drawer of the desk and pulling out piles of papers with shaking hands. And as they slid onto the desk she fanned them out and saw photographs of the fields she knew so well, fields she had walked across since she was a child, the pub where Lorenzo had kissed her that night, the river where her father had taken her to fish for trout, and where he had taken his life.

There was no need to look at any more. The evidence was all there. Clumsily she bundled the papers back up and shoved them into the drawer, then leaned on the desk for a moment, breathing hard.

So that was it. The silent, stalking beast had pounced. She

was caught in its claws, her heart ripped out, and the stupid thing was she wasn't even surprised.

She had known it was too perfect to be real.

Men didn't notice Sarah Halliday; she just wasn't that kind of girl. In a crowded room their eyes slid over her without interest as they looked for the next slim blonde. In particular, powerful, successful men like Lorenzo Cavalleri didn't notice her, and they certainly didn't single her out, take her out to lunch, look after her when she was tired, feed her cake and champagne, make her feel like a goddess, *unless they had a reason.*

Tears were running down her face, swiftly and silently falling onto the cluttered surface of Lorenzo's desk. Closing her eyes, she took a very deep breath, holding it for as long as she could, struggling to control the shadowy beast that now threatened to annihilate her. Her lungs burned and strained, and she exhaled slowly, then did it again.

There. It wasn't so bad. In and out, that was all there was to it. Now she just had to keep it up for the next sixty years or so.

The thought made her feel eerily calm and blank. Her face was wet but composed as she sat stiffly down on the chair again and picked up the telephone with numb fingers to book herself and Lottie on a flight back to England.

And then she took a blank sheet of paper from the tray on the desk and put it on the blotter in front of her, biting her lip hard as she began,

*Dear Lorenzo…*

# CHAPTER SEVENTEEN

'HAPPY birthday, darling! Oh, goodness me, I hardly recognised you, you look so very grown-up now that you're *six!*'

Lottie turned her cheek resolutely away from her grand-mother, so Martha's kiss missed it and ended up somewhere above her ear. Sarah gave an apologetic shrug and smiled wanly.

Martha gave Lottie a robust hug. 'Go and find Grandpa in the other room and see what goodies he's got for you,' she said in a hearty, encouraging voice. Lottie said nothing, but walked listlessly to the door and disappeared.

'Sorry about that.' Sarah turned away and absent-mindedly rubbed at a stain on the cracked Formica worktop with a cloth. 'It's not personal. Not to you, anyway. It's just me she hates.'

'Oh, darling.' Martha's tone was both gentle and reproach-ful. 'She doesn't hate you, but it's understandable that she's upset. She was so happy at Castellaccio, and she loved Dino and Lupo, and Lorenzo...'

'Yes, well,' Sarah rubbed harder, 'that's the trouble with love, isn't it? It makes you happy for about five seconds and then it all goes horribly wrong. Perhaps the one good thing that'll come out of this is that she'll learn that at an early age. Love hurts. It's a useful lesson.'

Martha came to stand beside her and gently took the cloth from her hands. 'Sarah, what happened? I thought you were happy there too.'

The mark was still there, but Sarah dimly remembered that it always had been. Funny how in a few short weeks she'd forgotten the grimness and squalor of her own flat. It seemed incredible now that at one point she'd genuinely believed she might not come back here.

Ha. *And they all lived happily ever after…*

'I was,' she said in a low voice. 'I was happier than I thought it was possible to be.'

'So, what went wrong?'

The compassion in Martha's eyes was almost more than Sarah could bear. Clenching her jaw, barely moving her lips, she said, 'It was based on a total delusion. I thought he…liked me, for *me*.'

'So what makes you think now he didn't?'

Sarah had to laugh at that. It was a harsh, ugly sound in the small, shabby kitchen. 'It was all going so well up until the moment I found out he was banking on me giving him the film options to Dad's book. He did a very good job of making it look like he cared for me…' She stopped for a moment, horror closing in on her as her mind scrambled back over it. Again and again, she did this. Remembering things he'd done or said that all made sense now. Like the night in the temple when she'd been so touched that he'd held her and talked to her about her father. God, she'd even thought that it meant *more* that he hadn't tried to get her clothes off…

Her eyes burned as she looked back up at her mother now. 'I can even tell you the exact moment when he realised. It was that first night, after the disaster with the roof and everything, and you introduced yourself.'

Bewildered, Martha shook her head. 'What are you talking about?'

'He knew who we were. He knew all about us. He'd been planning to make this film for ages.' She gave a strangled sob. 'I thought it was such a coincidence that we'd seen him in The Rose and Crown, but it wasn't. He was there checking out the location, and then when we all turned up on his doorstep I bet he couldn't believe his luck. No wonder he let Angelica get married there. No wonder he singled me out especially. He knew that I held the rights to the book. He knew…' she faltered, and took a gasping breath '…he knew my *real* name.'

'Oh, Sarah…'

'So you see, I couldn't stay. I know it was cowardly to run away without talking to him, but it would have been just too humiliating and painful, to have to face him and tell him that I knew it was all lies…'

Martha's shoulders sagged with the enormity of it all. 'Does he know yet that you're gone? Have you heard from him?'

'No. Not from him. I got a call yesterday from someone called Jim at this film studio. He's a friend of Lorenzo's, and he was very nice and very gentle and sympathetic and told me that Lorenzo had organised this treat for Lottie today, and that he hoped we would still be able to come "despite what had happened".' Sarah couldn't keep the sour sarcasm from her voice. 'So Lorenzo might not have spoken to me, but it seems he's spoken to this Jim.'

'He got in touch with us last week about today,' Martha said flatly. 'Guy and I were saying how much trouble he'd gone to, and we were so happy because we thought it must mean—'

'I know,' Sarah cut in harshly. 'I did too. But it didn't, did it?'

At that moment the door burst open and Guy appeared with Lottie on his back. He was wearing a sequinned tiara and was carrying a fur-trimmed wand, which he was waving around frantically as he pretended to look for her.

'Has anyone seen the birthday girl? Because unless I'm very much mistaken we have to leave in a moment for a birthday surprise at a mystery location, and if I can't find her she's going to miss it.'

'Here I am!' Lottie cried with something of her old sparkle as she waved her arms in front of Guy's face. But when Sarah caught her eye and smiled she looked away.

\* \* \*

'*Grazie,* Jim. I appreciate this.'

Jim took the package that Lorenzo handed him and gave a small shrug. 'Hey, anything to oblige. I know how important this girl is to you, and if I can smooth the path of true love *and* secure us the go-ahead for the film, then, man, I'll do anything.'

'She's given me the rights,' Lorenzo said tonelessly. 'And her blessing.'

Lorenzo turned away. The letter was in the inside pocket of his jacket, and he touched it with his fingertips now. For reassurance. There was no need to read it again; he already knew it virtually by heart.

> *The rights to the book are yours. You seem to be able to take the most unpromising, easily overlooked material and turn it into something that feels special, so I know that you'll treat it with respect and tenderness. I know this because it's how you have treated me, although you were never honest about your motives for doing so.*

'That's great! Isn't it?' Jim clapped his hands and rubbed them together.

Lorenzo winced, pressing his temples and trying hard to control the savage desperation that was tearing his insides apart. 'I don't just want the rights on paper. I want them morally, emotionally…' he said through gritted teeth. A yawning abyss lay in front of him, and he couldn't bring himself to look into it. 'I can't make this film unless she's with me.'

'But you said she gave you her blessing. What more do you want?'

Lorenzo turned round, and his face was a frozen continent of despair.

'Her.'

Film studios, it seemed, were like so much else in life. Glamorous and exciting in theory, but disappointingly scruffy and dingy in reality.

'The moon!' shrieked Lottie, clapping her hands. She was standing up, her face dimly illuminated in the bluish light, an expression of absolute wonder upon it that made Sarah's heart turn over. On the screen in front of them the tiny crescent of a new moon appeared. Sarah saw Lottie and Dino look at each other with wide eyes, linking hands and screwing up their faces intently as they made a wish.

The moon got bigger. It felt as if you were there, standing in space, staring out into the vast, starry expanse of eternity. Sarah recognised some of the shots from the Galileo film, and that above all else seemed to bring Lorenzo painfully close. His vision. His amazing creative talent. She was taut as a bow string, her hands balled tightly into fists as the film continued its journey around the heavens, and she was desperate for it never to end. She just wanted to keep watching the vision that Lorenzo had created, because the moment it was over he would be gone and it would be like saying goodbye to him all over again.

But it did end. The stars dimmed. The room went dark and she felt herself collapse inside a little, breathless and dejected.

Then a white square leapt across the black screen in front of them, numbers scrolling across it, like on an old-fashioned movie reel. The music that Sarah recognised from hearing so many times floating out from Lorenzo's study at the *palazzo* suddenly filled the small room, and Lottie appeared on the screen. Lottie, in her bridesmaid dress, stepping daintily down the stairs at Castellaccio.

The footage was jerky, deliberately naïve, the camera zooming in on her face as she flashed a mischievous smile into the lens. A little murmur of appreciation went round the room at this surprise, and at Lottie's sweetness, and, glancing at her, Sarah saw the delight on her face at being the star of her own film.

And then the screen blurred and the music slowed and quietened, until it was just one unbearably poignant violin. Instead of Lottie, Sarah found she was looking up at herself. A black and white image of herself, wrapped in a towel, her hair wet around her shoulders as she leaned over the banister at the *palazzo,* spread across a twelve-foot screen.

Anguish sliced through her. Her hands went up to her face, half-covering her eyes. She felt paralysed with horror, pinioned with shame at the thought of everyone watching her, and willed the moment to be over and the camera to shift to something else.

But it didn't.

It lingered on her face, closing in, picking up the play of emotions there as she watched the scene below. Sarah remembered it clearly; Angelica leaving for her wedding with Lottie, solemn and exquisite at her side, and she saw her own wistful joy, her pride in her daughter. The film slowed, the camera clearly picking up the tears that shimmered in her eyes as she blew a kiss down.

More. There was more. She was walking across the lawn in her lilac dress, her feet bare, her hair loose. Running down the stairs at the *palazzo,* saying something over her shoulder and smiling. Getting out of the car, her arms full of shopping, the keys clamped between her teeth. And there were still photos of her too, bending over and talking to Lottie; laughing with a glass of wine in her hand, sunlight slanting across her face; blowing a bubble from Lottie's bubble wand, her lips pouting as if in a kiss.

Of her in Venice, a Press shot from the red carpet. Hand in hand with Lorenzo as they got out of the car.

Another, taken a few seconds later. A close-up of her looking up into the sky as he leant close and whispered in her ear.

Oh, God.

It was like a love letter. A love letter in images.

Around her everyone was very still; every pair of eyes in the room was trained on the screen.

Another shot. Close up at first. Very close. Eyes closed, lashes sweeping down over her cheeks, then moving out to show her mouth, her lips slightly parted, her hair spilling out across the pillow. Oh, dear lord, Lorenzo must have taken it when she was in his bed at Castellaccio. She was sleeping and she looked peaceful and happy and...almost...yes, almost...

'Now can you see it? Now do you understand?'

She gasped. His voice was a broken rasp of despair beside her in the darkness, and he was taking her hands, squeezing tightly as he said so quietly that no one else could hear, 'You're *beautiful,* Sarah, you're so beautiful…can you see it now?'

'Oh, God, Lorenzo…'

'Shh,' he moaned, pressing his fingertips to her lips. 'You have to let me apologise. You have to let me explain, please. About the film.'

Around them everyone else was still watching the screen, oblivious. Tears spilled down Sarah's cheeks, blurring the images in front of her eyes. 'It's all right,' she whispered, 'you don't have to.'

'I do,' he said in a low, fierce voice. The dark enfolded them, so that she couldn't see his hands holding hers; could only feel the strength of his grip and sense his despair. 'I wanted to do it before I met you. For years. It was a dream…' He broke off, and in the flickering light from the screen she saw the abject torment on his face. She gave a sob, pressing her face into his chest to muffle the sound, not wanting to draw anyone's attention.

'Why didn't you tell me?'

His mouth was against her hair, his voice cracked with pain. 'At the beginning it was because I wanted to work out the best way to approach you. But as time went on it became so much more important than that. I was so scared of not getting it right. Of letting you down. I wanted to show you how brilliant your father was, in the hope that it might help you to see how brilliant you are…'

Against the darkness of his chest she closed her eyes and breathed him in, wanting to absorb his essence and his strength into herself. Gently he took her face between his hands and tilted it up towards him. His eyes were wet with tears and full of agony.

'And you are brilliant. You fill my head and you make things make sense and you inspire me, so that I don't care if I never make another film again, just as long as I can have you and tell you every day for the rest of my life how beautiful you are and how much I love you.'

Weak with relief and joy, scarcely able to take in that he was there, never mind what he was saying, she grasped blindly at the collar of his jacket. He bent his head and kissed her with a ferocious, bruising tenderness, crushing her against him while his lips moved across her trembling mouth, her wet cheeks, her eyelids, her jaw…

The film had ended and the lights slowly came up again. Martha and Paola were hastily brushing tears from their cheeks, grinning self-consciously at each other. Lottie, thrilled and mellowed into forgiveness, instinctively looked round for her mother after three days of freezing her out, and gave a sudden, heart-rending sob.

'Lorenzo! Oh, *Lorenzo!*'

She hurtled towards him, and he and Sarah pulled apart just in time for him to catch her and hoist her into his arms. 'That's what I wished for when I saw the new moon!' she cried. 'I wished for *you*. And Lupo. Did you bring him?'

Lorenzo shook his head and caught Sarah's eye, with an expression that made her heart turn over. 'I thought I'd planned everything, but you thought of the one thing I'd forgotten.' He kissed her cheek and buried his face in her hair. 'Is there anything else you wished for that I could give you instead?'

Lottie put her head on one side and gave a coy, dimpled smile. 'A new daddy? And to live next door to Dino for ever…'

Lorenzo laughed, pulling Sarah into his arms so that both of them were folded into the strength and safety of his body. He dropped his head so he could look into Sarah's eyes, and she caught the low note of hope and longing in his voice as he said, 'Well?'

'Yes.' She was crying and smiling as she pressed her mouth to his. 'Oh, yes, please.'

# EPILOGUE

*'IT WAS widely agreed that the wife of director Lorenzo Cavalleri, who was awarded Best Director for* The Oak and the Cypress, *easily outshone many of Hollywood's more polished stars with her lustrous natural look...'*

Smiling broadly, Lorenzo leaned back against the pillows and stroked a leisurely hand down Sarah's bare back as he turned the newspaper over and read further down the column:

*'Sarah Cavalleri was radiant in a midnight-blue Valentino dress that looked slightly more crumpled than when it appeared on the catwalk in Milan last month, and the trademark necklace of diamond stars that she has worn at all her public appearances. The 31-year-old's naturally curly hair was loose about her shoulders, and it appeared to be still wet as she walked up the red carpet hand in hand with her husband. Experts also speculated that her glowing skin had more to do with diet and exercise than make-up...'*

'Oh, God,' Sarah yelped and buried her head in the duvet. Lorenzo laughed and carried on.

*'Her seemingly effortless beauty has been rapturously heralded as the start of a backlash against increasingly extreme A-list perfection.'*

'Stop!' she croaked, moving the corner of the duvet back so she could look at him from beneath it. 'It doesn't really say that, does it? About my dress being creased and my hair still being wet?'

Lorenzo let the paper drop as he kissed her bare shoulder. Thin spring sunshine was pouring through the windows of the hotel's penthouse suite, glinting on the gold statuette that stood on the dressing table and illuminating the chaos in the luxurious room. The midnight-blue dress was now discarded on the floor, along with Lorenzo's white evening shirt and bow tie, and Sarah's shoes.

'Oh, yes, it does,' he murmured appreciatively against her warm skin. 'You're famous, *tesoro*.'

Sarah groaned. 'Famous for being the woman who was so busy being thoroughly seduced by her multi-talented husband, *in her award-ceremony dress,* ten minutes before the car came that she didn't have time to put on make-up.'

'No. Famous for being beautiful. And they were right about the exercise,' he said huskily, trailing a finger across her collar bone. 'You do realise you're going to be inundated with requests from magazine editors wanting to know your beauty secrets now?'

She propped herself up on her elbows, smiling wickedly into his eyes. 'The trouble is that none of them are remotely suitable for publication. What else does it say?'

'Nothing important.' He kissed the hollow beneath her jaw, and the newspaper slid from his fingers. Sarah caught it before it fell to the floor.

'Uh-uh, not so fast,' she said huskily. 'I want to hear the bit about how brilliant you are...'

Lorenzo carried on kissing her as she sat up properly and started to read.

*'Collecting the ceremony's most prestigious award, Lorenzo Cavalleri paid tribute to Francis Tate—author of the book on which his film is based and his wife's late father—thanking him for "giving the world an extraordinarily beautiful book" and for "giving me my extraordinarily beautiful wife and daughter…"'*

Sarah's voice cracked and she faltered for a second, before carrying on in a choked voice.

*'Cavalleri, who is known in the industry for his inscrutable calm, seemed to struggle for a moment to keep his emotions in check in what was, despite its unusual brevity, undoubtedly one of the most moving speeches of the evening.'*

She stopped, her eyes shimmering with tears, remembering the moment when her husband had stood in front of the packed auditorium and a worldwide television audience of millions and gazed down at her, lost for words, the huge screen behind him magnifying the expression of profound love on his face.

'It was…wonderful,' she sighed softly, running her fingers through his hair with infinite tenderness.

'I didn't mean it to be quite so brief,' he admitted gruffly, capturing her hand in his and dropping a kiss into the centre of her palm. 'There were lots of other people I should have thanked. Most notably you.'

'You don't have to thank me for anything.'

He took her face between his hands, his eyes searching hers, searing into her soul as the smile died on his lips. 'I have you to thank for…*everything*. If I'd started it would have taken all night.'

There was a pause, a heartbeat, as the atmosphere between them shifted and intensified and their locked gazes darkened. 'As I recall,' Sarah breathed, 'it pretty much did…'

'Hmm,' Lorenzo murmured as he pulled her into his arms, 'and I've barely even scratched the surface…'

## HARLEQUIN *Presents*

## PREGNANT BRIDES

*Inexperienced and expecting,*
*they're forced to marry!*

Bestselling Harlequin Presents author

# Lynne Graham

brings you the second story
in this exciting new trilogy:

## RUTHLESS MAGNATE, CONVENIENT WIFE
### #2892
*Available February 2010*

Also look for

## GREEK TYCOON, INEXPERIENCED MISTRESS
### #2900
*Available March 2010*

# TWO CROWNS, TWO ISLANDS, ONE LEGACY

*A royal family torn apart by pride and its lust for power, reunited by purity and passion*

Harlequin Presents is proud to bring you the final installment from The Royal House of Karedes. As the stories unfold, secrets and sins from the past are revealed and desire, love and passion war with royal duty!

Look for:

## THE DESERT KING'S HOUSEKEEPER BRIDE
### #2891

*by Carol Marinelli*
*February 2010*

# REQUEST YOUR FREE BOOKS!

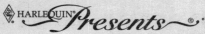 HARLEQUIN® *Presents* ®

## 2 FREE NOVELS
## PLUS 2
## FREE GIFTS!

**YES!** Please send me 2 FREE Harlequin Presents® novels and my 2 FREE gifts (gifts are worth about $10). After receiving them, if I don't wish to receive any more books, I can return the shipping statement marked "cancel". If I don't cancel, I will receive 6 brand-new novels every month and be billed just $4.05 per book in the U.S. or $4.74 per book in Canada. That's a savings of close to 15% off the cover price! It's quite a bargain! Shipping and handling is just 50¢ per book*. I understand that accepting the 2 free books and gifts places me under no obligation to buy anything. I can always return a shipment and cancel at any time. Even if I never buy another book, the two free books and gifts are mine to keep forever.

106 HDN EYRQ   306 HDN EYR2

| | |
|---|---|
| Name | (PLEASE PRINT) |
| Address | Apt. # |
| City | State/Prov. | Zip/Postal Code |

Signature (if under 18, a parent or guardian must sign)

### Mail to the **Harlequin Reader Service:**
**IN U.S.A.:** P.O. Box 1867, Buffalo, NY 14240-1867
**IN CANADA:** P.O. Box 609, Fort Erie, Ontario L2A 5X3

Not valid to current subscribers of Harlequin Presents books.

**Are you a current subscriber of Harlequin Presents books and want to receive the larger-print edition? Call 1-800-873-8635 today!**

\* Terms and prices subject to change without notice. Prices do not include applicable taxes. Sales tax applicable in N.Y. Canadian residents will be charged applicable provincial taxes and GST. Offer not valid in Quebec. This offer is limited to one order per household. All orders subject to approval. Credit or debit balances in a customer's account(s) may be offset by any other outstanding balance owed by or to the customer. Please allow 4 to 6 weeks for delivery. Offer available while quantities last.

**Your Privacy:** Harlequin Books is committed to protecting your privacy. Our Privacy Policy is available online at www.eHarlequin.com or upon request from the Reader Service. From time to time we make our lists of customers available to reputable third parties who have a product or service of interest to you. If you would prefer we not share your name and address, please check here. ☐

HP09R

# HARLEQUIN *Presents*

## EXTRA

**Presents Extra brings you
two new exciting collections!**

## LATIN LOVERS
*They speak the language of passion!*

**The Venadicci Marriage Vengeance** #89
by MELANIE MILBURNE

**The Multi-Millionaire's Virgin Mistress** #90
by CATHY WILLIAMS

## GREEK HUSBANDS
*Saying "I do" is just the beginning!*

**The Greek Tycoon's Reluctant Bride** #91
by KATE HEWITT

**Proud Greek, Ruthless Revenge** #92
by CHANTELLE SHAW

*Available February 2010*

I ♥ HARLEQUIN® *Presents*

# BROUGHT TO YOU BY FANS OF
# HARLEQUIN PRESENTS.

We are its editors and authors
and biggest fans—and we'd
love to hear from YOU!

**Subscribe today to our online blog at**
# www.iheartpresents.com